Tracks in the Sand

Western Stories

Other Five Star Titles
by H. A. DeRosso, edited by Bill Pronzini:

Under the Burning Sun (1997)
Riders of the Shadowlands (1999)

Tracks in the Sand

Western Stories

H. A. DeRosso

edited by
BILL PRONZINI

Five Star
Unity, Maine

Additional copyright information on page 216.

All stories were edited by Bill Pronzini
for publication in this collection.

Five Star First Edition Western Series.
Published in 2001 in conjunction with
Golden West Literary Agency.

Set in 11 pt. Plantin by Minnie B. Raven.

Printed in the United States on permanent paper.

Library of Congress Cataloging-in-Publication Data

DeRosso, H. A. (Henry Andrew), 1917–1960.
Tracks in the sand : Western stories / by H.A. DeRosso ; edited by Bill Pronzini.
p. cm.
ISBN 0-7862-2400-2 (hc : alk. paper)
1. Western stories. I. Pronzini, Bill. II. Title.
PS3507.E695 T73 2001
813′.54—dc21 00-054257

Table of Contents

Foreword

TRACKS IN THE SAND was Henry Andrew DeRosso's first published novel. It originally appeared in 1951 under the imprint of Readers Choice Library, a short-lived and poorly distributed paperback publisher. Like much of his long fiction of the 1940s and early 1950s, it is not so much a straightforward narrative as a series of set-piece scenes played out on a surreal, mythical landscape and peopled by desperate individuals—most notably its protagonist, a hard-shell loner named Blackwell—who lead grim and often doomed lives. This short novel's nightmare vision, its unrelenting pace, raw violence, and stark imagery, make it a compelling reading experience.

The remaining four tales in these pages demonstrate other facets of DeRosso's talent. "The Longest Ride" is reflective of the deep-felt sentiment that leavens his somber worldview. Poignant and satisfying, it is the account of a champion rodeo rider's struggles to overcome a devastating leg injury, his fear of being thrown again from a horse, and the pain caused by a crumbling marriage. "A Time for Rifles" is set in the author's native Wisconsin in the present day, yet this elemental, darkly realistic tale of two men and a woman on a fateful hunting trip is distinctly Western in tone; it might just as effectively have been set in an historical Far West milieu. "Look for the Blue Roan," one of two DeRosso stories to appear in the well-regarded *Zane Grey's Western Magazine*, edited by Don Ward, involves a young, inexperienced deputy sheriff with a stage hold-up, the man accused of the crime, and the man's fiercely loyal sister. The final entry, "The Scalp Hunters," was not published until ten years after DeRosso's tragic death in 1960 at the age of forty-three. It first appeared in *Long John Latham's Western Magazine*, under the pseudonym John Cortez. A grim tale of revenge and retribution, it features a pair of typically disaffected lead characters—a white man and an Apache woman. The background here is genuinely historical rather than mythical: the Arizona desert near the Mexican border, "the lonely land . . . the cruel vastness of desolation . . . the ancient home of [the Apaches'] ancestral fury."

TRACKS IN THE SAND is a worthy successor to UNDER THE BURNING SUN and RIDERS OF THE SHADOWLANDS, the previous two collections of H. A. DeRosso's uniquely *noir*ish brand of Western fiction.

Bill Pronzini
Petaluma, California

Tracks in the Sand

Chapter One

For all that day Blackwell had the feeling that he was being followed. It was nothing tangible so far as Blackwell could tell. Although he stopped every now and then to scan his back trail, there was nothing he could see that appeared to be out of the ordinary.

He supposed it was the complexion of the country through which he was passing that was having this effect on him. All about Blackwell loomed the heights of the Granadas. For two days now he had been traveling through the massive mountain range, and in that time he had not seen a single human being nor any sign of human habitation.

There was only silence, awesome and solemn and at times even forbidding, broken only by the clash of a shod hoof of the blaze-faced, white-stockinged bay against a stone or by a small, mournful squeak of saddle leather as he shifted his weight in the kack. The mountain slopes were covered with the green growth of pines and junipers. The highest peaks of the Granadas were barren, thrusting up bleak and ragged against the brazen sky.

Blackwell was not surprised that these mountains were devoid of human occupancy. There was little to beguile a man into settling down here. Outside of the junipers and pines there was only the ubiquitous sage and mesquite and hardly any graze whatever. A man would be crazy to settle here unless there were gold or silver in the bowels of the mountain, and of this Blackwell knew nothing for his business was the raising and marketing of cows and not the finding of hidden wealth.

Despite the apparent desolation, he could not shake the

sensation that he was not alone. If there were others here, they had as much license as he to be in the mountains. But the thought persisted in him that whatever presence existed here was for him. He kept getting uneasier right along.

This idea of seeing nothing ominous, of only feeling it, of knowing that it was out there somewhere beyond his ken, of believing that whatever it was boded him no good, finally made Blackwell irritable and mean. He could feel it chilling the back of his neck, now and then. He could sense its menace in a sudden, convulsive knotting of his entrails, the tightening of the muscles of his thighs.

Tom Blackwell was twenty-six years old. He was six feet tall, and he weighed one hundred and seventy pounds which made him rather lean. But what he had worked at all his life had given him little time to lie around and put on weight. His calling showed in the flat leanness of his hips and in the rope burns on his hands. Blackwell knew cattle, and beyond that he cared very little.

On his head he wore a gray, high-crowned Stetson with a crease in the front and with the brim curled up a little on the sides. He had on a black, double-breasted shirt and over this a blue denim, flannel-lined jumper. His Levi's were protected by a pair of black, flaring chaps. He wore plain, black, high-heeled boots that were trailed by the only ornate thing about him—a pair of large-roweled, silver-plated spurs. A black shell belt, every loop filled with .44s, slanted across Blackwell's waist. The belt supported a holster that held a .44 Colt Frontier six-shooter with a seven-and-a-half inch barrel.

Blackwell had not shaved in two days, and a dark stubble now lined the gaunt planes of his cheeks. His nose was long and aquiline. His lips had thinned while he drew pensively on his cigarette. His eyes, ordinarily a mild brown, were gelid and grimly appraising while he studied the land below and beyond him.

Once Blackwell thought he caught a glimpse of something. His heart pounded a little faster while he squinted his eyes still more. He leaned forward slightly and stared as hard as he could, but, if there had been something, it was not repeated. But that dull, ominous certainty inside him persisted.

Late that afternoon, Blackwell passed a couple of flocks of grazing sheep and suddenly the mountains weren't so lonely and desolate any more. A weight seemed to lift from him, and he did not mind so much that feeling of being followed.

Just before nightfall he reached a small village that, Blackwell was told, was called San Felipe. The brown adobe buildings were set on a long, gentle slope. There was no shape or pattern to the town. Each building seemed to have been constructed just where it had stood, the fancy of its builder. The streets were erratic, merely winding, twisting ways about the buildings with no thought to pattern or purpose.

Blackwell queried and was told that there was an inn in the village run by one Domingo. He finally found the place. It was a sprawling structure with a touch of Pueblo architecture in its shape. Across the front of it someone had painted with black tar the words—**La Fonda del Reyes—Inn of the Kings**.

Blackwell went inside. He found a man seated on a stool in front of a fireplace, warming his hands over the flames. The man jumped to his feet when he heard the jingle of Blackwell's spurs and turned a widely smiling, expectant face up to Blackwell.

"Welcome to La Fonda del Reyes," the man said. "I, Domingo, greet you. What will be your pleasure, *señor?*"

"I want a room," said Blackwell.

"Oh, I have the most exquisite room!" exclaimed

Domingo, making delicate gestures with his hands.

"I only want something with a bed in it," said Blackwell wearily. He had not realized until now how tired he was. For several nights he had slept outside. Now he was looking forward to a room with a bed and a roof overhead. . . .

Blackwell went up to his room, feeling comfortable and at peace with everything. His belly was full of a good, hot meal that Domingo's wife had prepared. The bite of peppers and spices still burned the inside of his mouth a little but he had washed everything down with good wine, and he relished this slightly stinging aftertaste.

The wine had made him forget the tension and anxiety of that day. It also made him forget the somber reason for his presence here in the Granadas. There would be time enough to think of that on the morrow and in the days to follow. Right now Blackwell was just plain tired. He had a bed waiting, and he intended to make good use of it.

He lit the candle that was on a small, scarred chest of drawers and then shut the door. He removed first his Stetson and then his jumper. Next, he unbuckled the shell belt and holster and hung this on the brass bedstead. He removed his chaps and folded them and laid these, too, on the bedstead. It was then that he heard the door of his room opening.

It was being done so quietly and surreptitiously that Blackwell instantly remembered what he had felt that day. He did not turn to see who it was at the door. He reached swiftly instead for his gun in the holster hanging on the bedstead.

Blackwell's fingers had just touched the handle of the weapon when the voice said: "I wouldn't try it if I were you."

Blackwell pulled his fingers away. He was more startled than frightened, and he could not quite suppress a small gasp of surprise. The voice was that of a woman.

Slowly Blackwell turned. She was standing in the now

open doorway, appearing rather dim in the shadows, but the gun in her fist was distinct enough. It was a .41 Colt Lightning pistol. It was held steadily and threateningly in her hand, the muzzle gaping at Blackwell's chest.

The woman said: "Move away from your gun."

Blackwell did not stir. The astonishment was passing from him. In its place there came a strong curiosity. "What is this?" he asked.

The woman's voice thinned. "Will you move or will I have to blast you away from that gun?"

The tone of it sent a tiny, involuntary chill down Blackwell's back. Carefully he took two steps away from his holstered .44. He asked softly: "Is this far enough or do you want me to climb out of the window?"

"You're not one bit funny," said the woman. She stood there, tense and prepared. The .41 in her grip never wavered. It had followed unerringly Blackwell's sidewise movement.

In the flickering light of the candle, Blackwell could not see her too well. A stiff-brimmed, flat-crowned black hat was pulled down low, shading her face. From what he could distinguish of her features, Blackwell assumed that she was quite young. She was dressed in men's clothing—a flannel shirt topped by a fancy brown and white calfskin vest and worn buckskin *chivarras*. She moved slightly now, and the spurs on her heels jingled shrilly in the silence.

Blackwell said: "I've never been held up by a woman before, but I suppose there is a first time for everything."

"This is no hold-up."

"Oh?"

"What are you doing in the Granadas?" asked the woman.

Blackwell considered the question. He recalled that apprehensive feeling he had had during the day. He remembered Domingo's curiosity regarding the brand on the bay.

Now there was this woman. She sounded very serious and menacing. For the first time, he began to suspect that he was getting into something disturbing and involved.

Blackwell's eyes squinted slightly. "I'm just passing through," he said. "Why do you ask?"

She ignored his query. "Where are you from?"

"Timbuktu," said Blackwell.

He thought that she flushed. Then her voice came, quivering with ferocity. "If you know what is good for you, you'll answer my questions. Now tell me. Where are you from?"

"Why should that interest you?" asked Blackwell. "I don't know who you are. I never saw you before. Why should you want to know so much about me?"

"Because," said the woman, "I am trying to make up my mind whether I should kill you!"

She sounded sincere, ferally and frighteningly so. A chill laced the back of Blackwell's neck. He stared at the .41 with a new, taut respect. The muzzle went right on gaping hungrily at him.

"Why do you hate me like this," asked Blackwell, "when I don't even know you?"

She ignored this query, too. She said: "Your bay carries the Bar G Bar iron, doesn't it?"

"That's right."

"The Bar G Bar Ranch is in Colorado, isn't it?"

"Yes."

"What is your connection with Bar G Bar?"

Blackwell's eyes narrowed again. "Have you seen anybody from Bar G Bar in the Granadas? Have you had trouble with them?"

The woman said, lips moving stiffly: "I'm asking the questions."

"I'm asking some, too," said Blackwell with a little heat.

"Why don't you answer some of mine? Maybe then I'd answer some of yours."

"I'm holding a gun," said the woman. "You aren't. Now tell me. Why have you come to the Granadas?"

Blackwell drew a deep breath. He did not underestimate the delicateness of his situation. She was a woman, but she was purposefully determined. She had a gun on him, and he knew, from her attitude, that he could not afford to antagonize her too much. He believed that she would not be averse to using her .41.

"I suppose you've seen my bay?"

"I have."

Blackwell paused, then went on: "He's a beautiful horse, isn't he? I have a weakness for beautiful horses. What if I were to tell you that the bay isn't mine?"

"You were riding him," said the woman.

"Was that you following me in the Granadas today?"

The woman glowered a moment, then she said in a quiet, algid tone: "This is the last time that I'm going to remind you I'm asking the questions. Are you trying to say that you stole him?"

Blackwell raised a hand and rubbed at his chin. "You've sure got me in a pickle, ma'am. If I say the horse is mine, you'll probably kill me since you don't seem to like anybody connected with the Bar G Bar. If I say the horse isn't mine, then, if the law catches me, they'll put a rope around my neck and hang me for a horse thief. Either way I can't win, and I'd rather die from a bullet than from a stretched neck. So go ahead and shoot!"

The woman did not speak right away. She seemed to be considering everything very carefully, and finally she arrived at a decision.

"I'm not going to kill you . . . now. Before I go, I want to give you a bit of good advice. Go back to Colorado. Go back to your Bar G Bar. Get out of the Granadas. Of course, you can take a chance and stay if you're stubborn. All you can lose is your life."

"Will you tell me one thing before you go?" asked Blackwell. "What have you got against Bar G Bar? What has anybody from that outfit done to you?"

"I'm going to take your gun," she said, taking one step forward. "I'll leave it outside somewhere where you can find it. But don't follow me. Don't try anything funny. I may have told you I'm not going to kill you now, but I can always change my mind."

She came ahead, gun still covering Blackwell, and reached out and took his .44 from its holster on the bedstead. Then she began backing toward the door.

"Wait a minute," said Blackwell, getting angry. "Won't you tell me who you are? Won't you tell me what you've got against me and Bar G Bar?"

In the doorway, the woman paused. "Get out of the Granadas," she said, and went swiftly out the door, slamming it behind her.

Blackwell sprang for the door the instant it closed. The lock jammed for an instant, then he had it free and the door flung open. Blackwell raced out into the dimness of the corridor.

At the top of the stairs he found his .44 where it had been dropped by the woman. He paused to snatch up the weapon, then raced down the stairs. He saw no one downstairs but Domingo, again warming his hands over the flames in the fireplace.

Domingo looked up, astonished, as Blackwell, gun in hand, ran to the door of the inn. Only the darkness greeted Blackwell's gaze. There was nothing else for him to see.

Blackwell holstered his gun and went back into the inn. Domingo had his back turned. He seemed very preoccupied with the business of warming his hands.

Blackwell halted behind Domingo. Anger kept swirling inside him. "Where did that woman go?" he asked.

Domingo turned slowly and lifted wide, inquiring eyes. "Go?" he asked. "Woman?"

"Yes, yes," said Blackwell impatiently. "That woman who just ran through here. Where did she go?"

"There was no woman," said Domingo.

"She was dressed in men's clothing. She wore a brown and white vest and *chivarras*. Which way did she go?"

"I saw no one, *señor,*" said Domingo, spreading his hands expressively.

"Don't you give me that, too!" he shouted, reaching out and grasping the front of Domingo's white cotton shirt. He lifted Domingo up on his toes. "There was a woman who threatened to kill me. She must have come down these stairs. You saw her, Domingo. Who was she?"

Domingo swallowed hard. His paunch trembled with fright, but he was adamant. "You are mistaken, *señor*. There was no woman here, outside of my wife. There was no man, either. You are the only guest in La Fonda del Reyes tonight, *señor*."

A sense of futility swept through Blackwell. The conviction existed in him that Domingo had seen the woman, but Blackwell did not have the heart to force the man to admit it. Slowly he relaxed his grip on Domingo's shirt, and the man began hastily to shove his shirt back into his trousers.

Blackwell stood there, eyeing Domingo sternly. The man pretended not to notice this; he made a great display of arranging his shirt and trousers meticulously, but he could not effectively conceal his uneasiness.

Finally Blackwell said: "Had you ever seen the Bar G Bar brand before tonight?"

"Never, *señor!*"

"Are you sure?"

"I swear, *señor!*"

"There were two horses with that brand here in the Granadas two months ago. Those horses might still be here. Have you by any chance seen one or both of these *caballos?*"

Domingo stared sullenly at the floor. "I had never seen that brand until I saw it on your bay tonight."

It became apparent to Blackwell that he would get nothing more without resorting to violence, and he had already decided against that. So he said: "All right, Domingo. I don't know what's going on around here, but I aim to find out. When I do, I hope you won't be mixed up in it, because, if you are, I'm not going to forget that you lied to me."

Chapter Two

Blackwell came on the town of War Feather from the north. The trail wound down from a pass in the mountains, and even from a great distance he could see the sunlight shimmering and glimmering on the rooftops of the town. Up high like this, the town seemed much closer than it actually was. When Blackwell had attained the plain at the foot of the pass, he found that the town was still a long way off. He did not reach it until the middle of the afternoon.

There was not much reason for the existence of War Feather except that the S.P. tracks ran through the place. The land about it was desert. Sagebrush grew and here and there a Joshua tree thrust its green, spiny limbs at the yellow sky. Deep under the ground there was water, for several windmills clanked and creaked in the small wind coming down from the mountains.

Blackwell stopped at the first watering trough and let the bay drink its fill. He was covered with white dust from his journey. It seemed to him that the dust was not only on his clothing but also in his mouth and between his teeth and under his eyelids. While the bay drank, Blackwell dismounted and studied what he could see of the town through narrowed eyes, wondering again what sort of commerce kept the drowsy place alive. He had spotted several different brands on the cows he had come across while traveling through the mountains that day, and he supposed that War Feather was the most convenient shipping point. The loading pens by the railroad tracks seemed to indicate this.

When the bay's thirst was satisfied, Blackwell started up the street, leading the horse behind him. He walked slowly, searching for a stable. Most of the structures on this main drag were one-story, false-fronted affairs. There was one two-story building in the shape of an L at one intersection, and a sign proclaimed this edifice to be the **St. George Hotel**. Most of the structures of War Feather were of wood-frame construction, but there was also a smattering of low adobe buildings. They all looked sick and tired and very passive under the beat of the desert sun.

The main drag of War Feather was wide and straight. By standing in the middle of the street, one could look beyond both ends of it out into the glimmering desert. There were no walks. The dirt and sand of the street ran right up to the edges of the buildings.

Blackwell found his stable. He paid for a night's lodging for the bay and then headed for the St. George Hotel. He felt very tired and beaten, and he looked forward to washing up and lying down for a while. But then he remembered what he had come to this country for, and a nagging impatience filled him.

He supposed that the matter was not so pressing that he could not put it off a while longer. Yet he could not accept that thought. There was a premonition in Blackwell of a great unpleasantness ahead of him, and so he wanted to hurry about it to see if there was any substance to the prescience. He could not understand why he should feel this way.

He registered for a room at the St. George, and then, without going to the room, asked the clerk where he could find the sheriff's office. Then Blackwell went out on the street again.

On the way he passed several saloons, and his throat constricted eagerly at the thought of a cold glass of beer, but he did not stop in any of the places. Now that he felt he was close to what had brought him here, Blackwell had to exert an effort to keep his steps from quickening. His heart began to pound in a dull, leaden way.

The sheriff's office was off from the main street. Both the sheriff's office and county jail were housed in the same building, a thick, square, squat adobe structure. The ground was open all about the building. The nearest house was fifty feet away.

A door stood open, and from within came the sound of a sonorous snoring. Blackwell stepped into the dimness of the place, and squinted his eyes to see better in the gloom. The sheriff slept as peacefully as a child. He was a short man with thick shoulders and a thick middle. His hands were folded across his paunch, and his head was dropped back with the mouth slightly open, and with each exhalation of breath his lips fluttered. A bluebottle fly kept buzzing around, alighting every now and then on the sheriff's face and crawling around, but the man was impervious.

Blackwell reached forward and shook one of the sheriff's boots. The man muttered something unintelligible, gave a loud snort, and went right on sleeping. Blackwell shook harder.

This time the sheriff wakened. His eyes batted open and flickered wildly for several instants. His mouth worked and smacked dryly. He snorted and grunted and finally brought his head up enough so that he could glimpse Blackwell.

"Eh? Eh?" mumbled the sheriff. "What you want?"

"You Frank Richmond?" asked Blackwell.

"Yeh, yeh, that's me," said the sheriff, straightening up in the chair and dragging his feet off the table. His manner indicated that he did not like having his slumber disturbed. He yawned prodigiously and then began to scratch himself under the armpits.

"I want to ask you some questions about Jesse Gray," said Blackwell.

That took all the irritation and indifference out of the sheriff. He left off scratching and stared at Blackwell with a cool, grave intentness.

"Why should I tell you anything?" asked the sheriff.

"I'm Blackwell. I'm ramrod of Bar G Bar, Gray's ranch in Colorado. I'm representing Gray's widow."

The sheriff began to paw among the papers on his desk, but it was apparent that this was something new for a small layer of dust was on the top documents. "I believe I wrote a letter to Missus Gray. In that letter I explained everything I knew. Didn't you read that letter, Blackwell?"

"I did," said Blackwell. "That's why I came to War Feather. You didn't explain everything."

Richmond gave up the pretense of his interest in the papers. He settled back in the chair and began to scratch his side. "What didn't I explain?" he asked.

Blackwell did not answer this. He said: "How was Gray killed?"

"If you've read my letter, like you claim you've done, you know he was killed in a hold-up."

"What happened to the man who killed Gray?"

"That man is dead."

"Just like that?"

Richmond cocked his head to one side and stared hard at Blackwell. "I don't like the way you said that."

"I don't care what you like," Blackwell said thinly, and the sheriff flushed. "Who was this hold-up man who killed Gray?"

The sheriff wallowed around on his chair a moment. He seemed deeply in thought. He began scratching his chest absently.

At length, Richmond said: "I'll give it to you all at one time, the whole picture, everything I know, so you'll be satisfied and leave me alone. I'm a very busy man," he said blandly. "Like I said in my letter, Gray was killed up in the Granadas. That's my territory up there. Gray had another man with him, a Luke Chandler. You should know Chandler because he said he worked for Bar G Bar.

"Well, Chandler was with Gray, and he saw everything. This Mike Gómez, a young sheepman up there, holds up Gray. Gray resists. Gómez shoots him dead. Chandler doesn't make trouble, and so he doesn't get hurt. Gómez rides away. Chandler starts to ride for help, when he runs into two *hombres,* Tex Hogarth and young Bobby Sheppard. Chandler tells them his story, shows them Gray, and then all three of them ride to Gómez's place.

"Gómez is getting ready to quit the country. Hogarth and Sheppard try to stop him. Gómez starts to shoot, and Hogarth and Sheppard shoot back. Gómez gets killed. So then Chandler and Hogarth and Sheppard load Gómez and Gray on their bronc's and haul them into War Feather. There you have it, Blackwell, the whole thing."

"Stop fooling with those papers," said Blackwell sharply as the sheriff bent over his desk again. Richmond stiffened. "You still haven't finished telling me. Where's the money?"

"Money?" Richmond repeated, batting his eyes blankly.

A small anger began to stir in Blackwell. He was just starting to get an idea of what lay ahead of him. He had suspected something like this all along, but he had passed it off as an unnecessary worry. Now he was beginning to accept it for what it was—a long, ugly, and perhaps fruitless job.

"You said it was a hold-up," Blackwell said tightly. "A hold-up involves money, doesn't it? The hold-up man, this Gómez, was captured. So where is the money Gómez took from Gray?"

"Well," said Richmond, riffling several sheets of paper, his eyes turned down, "Gómez had forty-nine dollars on him."

"Forty-nine? That's a long way from eight thousand."

"Eight thousand?" Richmond echoed. "Did Gray have that much on him?"

"He sold a trail herd to the Fort Ridge Indian Agency. The Bar G Bar boys who came home on the train said that's what Gray was paid. Gray wrote a letter to his wife, saying he had heard there was some nice cow country down here in this territory and he wanted to look it over before he returned home. He sent the boys back, all but Luke Chandler. Gray took Chandler with him. Gray had the money on him. Where is it, Richmond?"

Richmond turned up the palms of his hands. "Don't ask me. I don't know."

"You're the sheriff, aren't you?" shouted Blackwell, losing his head. He leaned forward and slapped his hand down on the table. "What do you do when there is a hold-up and murder in your county? Sit on your rump and sleep?"

Richmond flushed. His eyes glittered with anger. "Could you do any better? Do you want my job? What do you think you could have done under the circumstances?"

Blackwell straightened and took a breath. He told himself it would not pay to keep losing his temper. He would not learn anything if he antagonized the sheriff. So Blackwell swallowed his anger and said in a more mollified tone: "Do you have any idea what might have happened to the money?"

The sheriff shrugged. "Gómez probably hid it. Now that he's dead it'll take a miracle to find it."

"If, like you said, Gómez was quitting the country, why would he hide the money? Wouldn't he take it with him?"

Richmond considered this for a moment. Then he shrugged again. "Gómez probably decided to run and stay away until things quieted down, and so he hid the money with the idea of coming back for it someday."

This did not sound very logical or convincing to Blackwell. He was about to inform Richmond of his opinion but then reconsidered and decided to let it pass. Blackwell had no doubt of Richmond's sincerity. The sheriff was just a lazy, incompetent man.

Blackwell tried another tack. "When did you see Gray?"

"I never saw him alive," said the sheriff. "Like I told you, Chandler and Hogarth and Sheppard brought in the two dead men, Gray and Gómez. Chandler identified Gray. He told me about Gray's wife and where to write to her. So we buried Gray, and I wrote the letter, and that's that." Richmond's eyes suddenly narrowed. "Say! You don't think Chandler has the money maybe?"

"I aim to find out," said Blackwell. "Is Chandler still around here? He never came home."

"Yeh, he's been hanging around War Feather and the Granadas. He worked a couple of weeks for Lazy S and then quit." He looked speculatively at Blackwell. "Personally, I think he's a poor bet for the money. Chandler sure don't act like he has it. He seems pretty much broken up about Gray's death. Drinks all the time. No," said Richmond, shaking his head, "Chandler isn't your man."

"I'll see about that," said Blackwell. He stared pensively at the far wall. "You mentioned Lazy S. Who owns that place?"

"Otis Sheppard."

"Sheppard. Any relation to this Bobby Sheppard you mentioned?"

"Otis Sheppard is Bobby's old man."

"I see." Blackwell, fingering his chin, gazed scornfully at the sheriff. "I suppose you didn't bother to check whether young Sheppard or this Hogarth has the money? They could have taken it off Gómez when they killed him."

Richmond made a derisive sound. "You don't think much of me, do you?" he asked, and then went on before Blackwell could answer. "Bobby Sheppard doesn't need money. His old man has more *dinero* than he knows what to do with. As for Tex Hogarth, he ramrods Lazy S and gets good pay for it. No, Blackwell. You're getting off on the wrong side of the horse."

The anger began to stir in Blackwell again. He had the feeling that he had learned as much as he would ever learn from the sheriff and it was far from satisfactory. If he wanted to learn any more, he was convinced he would have to find it out for himself without any help from Richmond. So Blackwell made no effort to suppress the wrath and disgust building up in him.

"You've got it all figured out conveniently, haven't you, Richmond? You've got it all figured out so you won't have to get up off your rump to do anything about it. Isn't that right?"

"Listen, Blackwell, I don't have to take any of this from you. I'll overlook it because I suppose you feel bad about what has happened to Gray, but you keep talking like this and I'll throw you in a cell back there until you cool off!"

"Think you can do it? Think you could get out of that chair long enough to try it?"

Blackwell, full of disappointment and disgust, turned away and started for the door. He had not reached the entrance, when Richmond said: "Why don't you forget it and go home, Blackwell? The thing is done. It's finished. The tally book is closed. Why don't you leave it that way?"

Blackwell turned in the doorway, one hand on the jamb. His voice was thick with anger. "There's a widow up in Colorado and a little boy who could sure use eight thousand dollars. Besides, it's rightly theirs. I'm getting that money for them if I have to tear the Granadas apart rock by rock."

Chapter Three

Blackwell went to his room in the St. George and slept the whole night through. He had a feeling that this would be the last night in a long while in which he could indulge in peaceful, undisturbed slumber, and so he made the most of it.

He awoke with the sun spearing through the window right on his bed, and it was this hot brightness on his face more than anything else that wakened him. He washed up and dressed slowly and then went downstairs. It was eight o'clock.

He passed through the lobby that was empty except for two cowpunchers seated in one corner. They looked Blackwell over carelessly as he passed, but he could not help but feel that there was more than indifference in their interest in him. He pretended not to notice them and passed outside. He had no idea who they were.

Blackwell stopped in a small lunchroom for breakfast. Soon after, the two cowpunchers of the St. George lobby entered and took seats at the other end of the counter. This time they showed no interest whatever in Blackwell, and this, instead of reassuring him, made him all the more uneasy.

He felt better with some food in him, and he had all but forgotten the two cowpunchers when he stepped outside again. He paused in the warm sun and built a smoke. Then he stood there, drawing on his cigarette, while he looked over the buildings on this main drag of War Feather, debating in his mind how to start going about his job. Then he crossed the street to the Longhorn Saloon.

The place was dim and cool. The heat had not yet begun

to penetrate the large barroom. Blackwell strode slowly up to the bar, his eyes squinted against the gloom.

The place was devoid of customers. Behind the bar stood a thin wisp of a man, a soiled apron around his skinny waist, wearily and resignedly polishing glasses. In the far end of the barroom was a swamper, making half-hearted passes with a broom. Pervading the air were the stale, sickly-sweet odors left over from the previous night's wassailing and hilarity.

The bartender was obviously suffering. His eyes were glazed and shot with red. He took great care in moving about so as not to bend and rise too abruptly. His hands trembled in the moment between setting down one glass and reaching for another. He did not seem very happy to have to wait on a customer this early in the morning.

Blackwell had intended buying a glass of beer which he could have had for a nickel, but then he decided that if he bought a shot of whisky for a dime the bartender might be more willing to impart information. So Blackwell ordered rye.

"How does an *hombre* go about getting out to Lazy S?" he asked.

That gave the barman pause. With a visible effort he put his suffering aside and frowned. "You don't know?"

"Would I be asking if I did?"

The bartender revolved the glass he was polishing slowly in his hands. "What you want with Lazy S?"

Blackwell swallowed his drink. He supposed that in a small town like War Feather his arrival here must be common news. He also had no doubt that the reason for his coming was known as well. Still, that shouldn't bring about a reluctance in answering his queries—unless there was something very wrong about the deaths of Jesse Gray and Mike Gómez.

"Are you going to tell me the way?" Blackwell asked softly,

trying to hold his temper in.

"If you're looking for a job, Lazy S ain't hiring nobody right now," said the bartender.

"That's right, Albert. Lazy S is full up with riders!"

Blackwell turned toward the door as these words were spoken. The two men had pushed through the batwing doors and were now coming up to the bar. They were the two cowpunchers of the St. George lobby and the lunchroom. There was no doubt of their interest in him now. They ignored Blackwell. They both ordered whisky and swiftly downed the drinks and immediately called for another round. Blackwell watched them with unabashed intentness.

The youngest was very loud, and his affected swagger bothered Blackwell. This young fellow did not appear to be more than nineteen or twenty. He was of medium height and slight of build, and he apparently tried to compensate for those fancied shortcomings through the use of a loud, offensive, and belligerent manner. His face was quite handsome, and he seemed fully aware of the fact. He had his cream-colored Stetson riding the back of his head. A lock of his tawny hair hung down over his forehead as if he went to great pains to achieve that effect.

He put away his second drink very quickly and called for another. He ordered another for his companion, too, but this one was more prudent. He had not yet downed his second shot, and he shook his head and placed his hand over his filled shot glass.

The second man appeared to be in his middle twenties. He was much more restrained in both mien and dress. Blackwell classed this second 'puncher as a very dangerous fellow. This man stood even taller than Blackwell, about six foot two. He was lean and gaunt. His thin face had a great predatory nose and a small, cruel mouth. Strange hard eyes seemed filled with a secret, scornful amusement.

He had an old, wide-brimmed, black felt hat set squarely on his head. His shirt was of blue denim, and over it he wore a black vest. His Levi's were worn and faded, especially at the knees and on the seat. Tied down low on his right thigh was a black-handled Remington .44-40. The weapon appeared to have seen a lot of use.

While the young 'puncher went on ignoring Blackwell, this second man turned now and frankly returned Blackwell's appraisal. Blackwell could feel himself being sized up and weighed and considered by that amused, hazel glance.

The young 'puncher downed his third shot with a casual flourish and then turned the full measure of his insolence on Blackwell. He looked Blackwell up and down, lips curling slightly. Then the kid said in what he fancied was a hard, fear-inspiring tone: "What you want with Lazy S, bucko?"

"I'm looking for a couple of Lazy S boys," said Blackwell quietly.

"What you want with them?"

"When I find them, I'll tell them."

The young fellow flushed. "We're Lazy S," he declaimed, smiting his chest. "Any business with Lazy S boys is our business. Me and Tex run Lazy S."

"Tex?" said Blackwell, staring at the tall 'puncher. "Would you be Tex Hogarth?"

The fellow inclined his head slightly. He said nothing.

Blackwell said to the young 'puncher: "I take it you're young Sheppard."

"You damn' right I am. Albert, give me another shot. Come on, Tex, drink up. You're falling behind."

Hogarth again placed his hand over his filled shot glass and shook his head. He never took his sardonic glance off Blackwell. Young Sheppard seized his shot glass and polished off the drink, then faced Blackwell again. "You ran off at the mouth with Richmond about me and Tex yesterday, Blackwell. You're going to get into trouble if you don't keep your trap shut!"

Although he tried to ignore it, the boy's insolence was getting at Blackwell. He felt a spasm of disgust.

"What did you do, Sheppard? Stand outside the door and eavesdrop?"

Young Sheppard flushed. "One of my boys was getting over a drunk in the jail. You talked loud enough so that he heard everything you said." Sheppard motioned the bartender to fill his glass once more.

Blackwell said: "That's just where you're going to wind up pretty soon yourself, sonny. Why don't you go easy? You've already proved to me that you can drink."

Rage darkened the boy's face. He took one step away from the bar so that his holstered gun hung free. Hogarth moved, too, coming out from behind young Sheppard and walking out to the middle of the barroom. This placed him to the left of Blackwell. Hogarth's eyes were amused.

Sheppard said loudly: "Are you going to apologize to us, Blackwell?"

Blackwell could see how it was building up. He did not want it like this. It wasn't that he was afraid. He would not accomplish anything by getting himself killed. When his time came, he would die without a whimper, but he had others to think about. He had to use great care right now. Still, he was not going to crawl.

"I have nothing to apologize for," Blackwell said quietly.

"You called me and Tex thieves. We don't take that from anybody."

Blackwell looked at Hogarth. The man stood with his right hand close to the handle of his Remington.

Blackwell's throat constricted a little. He shifted his attention back to the boy. "Listen, Sheppard," he said softly, mollifyingly. "I've got nothing against you or your pal. I never saw either of you before now, so how could there be anything between us? I'm here looking after the interests of Jesse Gray's family. Gray had eight thousand dollars on him when he was killed. I want to recover that money. I want to know where it is. Richmond told me that you and Hogarth killed Gómez who was supposed to have held up and robbed Gray. Yet Richmond says that Gómez had only forty-nine dollars on him when he examined the body. Where did the eight thousand go?"

"We ain't got it," said the boy. "You're a god-damn' liar, Blackwell, when you say we've got it!"

"I didn't say you've got it," said Blackwell through his teeth. "The way I've been given to understand, Gómez took the money from Gray, and a while later you and Hogarth killed Gómez. When Richmond saw Gómez's corpse, the eight thousand wasn't on it. Where did it go?"

"You're a dirty, stinking liar when you say we've got it," declared the boy hotly.

Blackwell slapped his left hand exasperatedly against his thigh. He could feel the anger rising. He did not want to yield to it but did not know how much longer he could contain himself. By giving into his wrath, he would be playing right into Sheppard's and Hogarth's hands. He did not have a chance against the two. They had him in a whipsaw. They could draw on him and fire at him from two directions. He would be lucky to get even one of them.

"Don't you have anything to say, Hogarth?" asked Blackwell. "All I want to know is what happened to that money. If Gómez didn't have it on him when you killed him, do you have any idea what he did with it?"

Hogarth's eyes glimmered with their private mirth. He shook his head.

"Can't you tell me anything?" asked Blackwell.

Again Hogarth shook his head.

Young Sheppard cried: "Are you yellow, Blackwell? Didn't you hear me call you a god-damn' liar?"

"All right," said Blackwell. He had been needled enough. He was not going to stand here and take the young squirt's rawhiding forever. "All right, kid, you want it and you'll get it. Your pal will likely get me, but not before I get you, you dirty, little, loud-mouthed squirt!" Blackwell's chest swelled. His right hand poised. He saw a flash of doubt and uncertainty cross young Sheppard's face.

Because he was concentrating so hard on his predicament, Blackwell was not aware of the batwings being shoved aside. Neither Hogarth nor Sheppard was conscious of this fact. Then a voice said: "I'm tired of waiting for you, Bobby."

That broke the spell. Young Sheppard emitted a sharp gasp of surprise and relief. The tenseness went out of Hogarth. His eyes lost some of their acute amusement. Both he and Sheppard turned on the one who had spoken.

Blackwell relaxed, too, with sweat lining the palms of his hands. He looked beyond Sheppard, and there he saw her.

She was standing there as if she were absolutely unaware of what she had interrupted. She had a tobacco sack and a paper in her hands, and her head was bowed as she gave all her attention to the pouring of a small trickle of tobacco on the paper. When this was done, she flicked the string of the sack between her teeth and with a swift yank jerked the pouch closed. Next she cropped the tobacco sack in a pocket of her shirt and raised her face and glanced fully at Blackwell. With one hand she rolled the tobacco paper into a tight cylinder, then, her eyes never wavering from Blackwell's, she daintily licked the rim of the paper and finished her cigarette.

"Will you give me a light, Bobby?" she said.

"You'd better go, Angel," said Sheppard. "Me and Tex got business here."

"Light my cigarette, Bobby," she said, voice hardening ever so slightly. The boy complied.

Her smoke lighted, she blew a great cloud of it, and through the fine, lifting haze she still watched Blackwell steadily. To Blackwell she was a very beautiful woman. Blonde hair hung down both sides of her face and brushed at her shoulders. She had rich, black brows, and under these her gray eyes were set wide apart. She had a rather long, thin nose and a wide mouth whose lower lip thrust out in an attractive, perpetual pout.

She was tall for a woman, about five foot nine, and Blackwell would have put her age around twenty-three or twenty-four. She was wearing a black and red checkered flannel shirt, and despite its looseness the fullness of her breasts was still apparent. She also wore a fringed buckskin divided riding skirt that reached just below her knees to the tops of small, fancy riding boots.

Blackwell felt something stir in him. He was not at all sure what it was—just the beginning of a sensation he had never before experienced when looking at a woman.

Young Sheppard was almost fawning in his attentions to the woman, and this struck a sudden, vehement resentment in Blackwell. He realized it was none of his business, but still he resented it. The woman paid only the slightest heed to the boy. Her eyes rested unswervingly on Blackwell. He could feel himself being taken apart and analyzed and put back together again by those cool gray eyes.

Finally the woman wrinkled her nose as she sniffed a little and said: "You think too much, Bobby. Get out of here."

The boy spread his hands. "But this is Blackwell, Angel. He. . . ."

"You talk too much," she said coldly. "Get out."

Hogarth spoke now. "Let's go, Bobby," he said quietly, starting for the door. Grumbling, the boy followed. They passed through the batwings, and then there was only Blackwell and the woman in the barroom.

Blackwell wanted to speak to her, but he did not know where to begin. The coolness and persistence of her stare disconcerted him. It was a frank unabashed consideration of him, and he began to feel uncomfortable and a bit angry. She kept drawing on her cigarette and blowing the smoke lazily through her lips and watching him through the haze. She did not say a word.

At last she finished. Dropping her cigarette to the floor, she ground it out with the toe of her boot. Then she turned and went out of the door. Blackwell went up to the batwings and watched her as she walked with a free-swinging stride down the main drag of War Feather.

He could hear the loud beating of his heart.

Chapter Four

Blackwell concluded that the best way he could get at the root of his problem would be to have a talk with Luke Chandler. Chandler had worked for Bar G Bar a number of years. He had got to be quite friendly with Jesse Gray. He had accompanied Gray from the Fort Ridge Indian Reservation here into the Granadas. Chandler had been present when Gray had been held up and killed. Chandler should know more about the matter of Jesse Gray's death and the disappearance of his money than anyone else, Blackwell decided.

Luke Chandler was not in War Feather. No one could tell Blackwell for sure where Chandler was. Almost everyone he asked agreed that Chandler most likely was somewhere in the mountains. Blackwell was told that Chandler had worked a short while for Lazy S but then had quit. Chandler had the reputation of a shiftless drunkard, and this Blackwell found hard to believe, for Chandler had never been a drinking man. Of course, grief over Jesse Gray's tragic death might be responsible. This might also explain why Chandler had never returned home. It was possible that the man could not bring himself to face Gray's widow and child after what had happened.

So Blackwell saddled his blaze-faced bay and rode up into the Granadas once more. He steered clear of Lazy S. It was not that he was afraid of Tex Hogarth and Bobby Sheppard. To the contrary, Blackwell now detested the two, and he knew that, if he encountered them again, he would not wait for them to begin badgering him again.

Blackwell found himself thinking every now and then of the blonde woman who had intervened so opportunely at the Longhorn Saloon. He just could not get her out of his mind.

She was a very attractive woman, and he supposed that might be the reason, but, when he really got down to it, he knew it was something more than that.

Her name was Angel Dawson. That much he had learned about her. She had come to War Feather about six months ago, and no one knew very much about her except that she ran around with Bobby Sheppard and was generally believed to be his girl even though she was several years older.

Blackwell passed from cattle country into sheep country in the Granadas without finding a trace of Chandler. This sheep country lay deeply in the mountains and existed around the hub of the little village of San Felipe that Blackwell remembered only too well. The graze in this part of the mountains was not as lush as that where beef was raised. The sheepherders were all of Spanish extraction and had been settled here two hundred years before the Anglo-Americans had come. Blackwell had no doubt that the relations between the two groups were not exactly amicable.

Blackwell came across a sheepherder who spoke English quite well. He asked his inevitable question as to whether the herder had seen Chandler. The herder had a long, sad face, and he leaned heavily on his staff while he stared up at Blackwell on his bay. In answer to the query the herder shook his head.

"Would you know Chandler if you saw him?" asked Blackwell.

"Sí, señor."

"Has he ever been up in this part of the Granadas?"

The herder dropped his glance to the Bar G Bar brand on the bay's rump. He seemed to be considering something very carefully. Finally he said: "Chandler would never come into this part of the mountains."

"Why not?"

"Can you not guess? It is because of Chandler that Miguel Gómez was killed." The herder shrugged. "There are many among us who do not believe that Miguel Gómez was guilty of the killing of your employer."

Mention of Gómez started another thread of thought in Blackwell's mind. The robbery and killing of Gray and then the killing of Gómez had always struck Blackwell as too pat and convenient. Something kept telling him that in the killing of Gómez lay the key to the whole puzzle.

He hipped around in the saddle and stared off unseeingly while he ran a few facts through his mind. He could hear the soft bleating of several lambs in the flock of sheep that was spread like a dirty gray blanket over a hillside. The cries were sad and forlorn. They were very much in keeping with the feeling in Blackwell's head this day.

Blackwell turned now and looked down at the herder. "Where is this place of Gómez?"

The herder waved a hand languidly in the direction from which Blackwell had come. "The place of Gómez is over there, next to the buildings of Lazy S. But the land no longer belongs to Gómez."

"Oh?" said Blackwell. "Didn't Gómez have any heirs?"

"He is survived by his mother, an old woman."

"Isn't she living in her home any more?"

The herder spread out a hand, palm upward. "The land is no longer hers. The place of Miguel Gómez now belongs to Lazy S."

"Oh?" said Blackwell again. For the first time since he had come into the Granadas things began to make a little sense. "Has there been much trouble between the sheep growers and the cattlemen here in the mountains?"

"Not until recently," said the herder. "We have always lived in peace. Long ago we reached an understanding. We sheep growers stick to our part of the mountains, the cattlemen to theirs. This agreement was kept by everybody until Lazy S broke it."

"Why did Lazy S break it?"

"Why are some men slaves of greed?" asked the herder. He shrugged. "The old *Señor* Sheppard is a good man who is content with what he has, but he takes little interest in Lazy S. It is the young *Señor* Sheppard who manages the affairs of Lazy S. One would not think that the young *señor* is the natural son of his father," said the herder.

"I know," said Blackwell bitterly. "Where is this mother of Miguel Gómez living now?"

The herder said nothing.

"I mean her no harm," said Blackwell. "I am here in the interests of Jesse Gray. He is survived by a widow and a small son. It is because of them that I am in the Granadas, *amigo*."

The herder stared a while longer at Blackwell, obviously trying to make up his mind. Finally he said: "I believe you are all right, *señor*. You are not like Chandler, so I will tell you. This, then, is how to arrive at the home of the mother of Miguel Gómez. . . ."

The place was an adobe hut on the banks of a small creek that wriggled its way through this part of the Granadas. Blackwell rode out of the pines and into the small open space about the hut. The place seemed deserted.

It was apparent that, until recently, this tiny house had been unoccupied. The thatched roof showed recent repairs, and the door had not long ago been re-hung on new hinges. But there was no indication that at the moment the hut was inhabited.

Blackwell dismounted and looked about him. He had the uneasy feeling that he was being watched, not from the house but from the trees out of which he had just come. He stared long and hard but could see nothing. He went to the door and knocked.

While he waited, Blackwell turned and again looked about him. Somewhere in the trees a lark was singing. The bay stamped a hoof fretfully as it grazed and switched its tail at the flies that were buzzing around its rump. Nothing sounded within the house.

Blackwell rapped again. Once more there was only silence. He seized the latch and tried the door and found it unbolted. He opened it, and after a moment stepped inside.

The woman was sitting with her back to the door, staring down into the ashes of a dead fire. She did not stir as Blackwell entered. He left the door open and took another step ahead, but the woman did not seem to hear. She went on staring into the ashes in the fireplace.

The thought came to him that the woman might be dead. Then he saw the cloth of her dress move ever so slightly as she breathed.

He said: "*Señora* Gómez?"

She raised her head a little, although she did not turn to look at him. "Who is it?" she asked wearily.

"You do not know me," he said. "My name is Blackwell."

He saw her shoulders stiffen. For a moment she did not speak. Then her voice came, full of anguish. "Why did you have to come? I know nothing. I am an old woman who has lost her only son. Go away and leave me alone."

Blackwell was not very much surprised that she had heard of him. He realized that his presence here in the Granadas and the reason for his coming were now probably known to everyone who was at all concerned with the deaths of Gray and Gómez. He stood there, awkwardly, hating every moment of this but determined to go through with it. He said gently: "I will not take up much of your time."

"Time?" she said. She swung around on her stool and turned her face up to Blackwell. It was an old face, worn and grooved with grief. The brown eyes were luminous with an old, incessant pain. "Time? What is time to me? I have nothing to do. I have nowhere to go. Time is nothing to me. Time means that I must sit and think of my Miguelito."

"I'm sorry," said Blackwell, feeling a thickness in his throat. "I don't like to bother you about it, but I am trying to learn something. You were his mother. You knew him better than any one else."

"Yes," she said, nodding her head continuously, her eyes downcast, staring at the floor and beyond the floor and seeing none of this, seeing only her deep, tormented memory. "What mother doesn't know her child better than anyone else?" Her right hand struck her breast over her heart. "He came out of here. His flesh was my flesh, his blood was my blood. He was my own Miguelito. Why shouldn't I grieve for him?"

She lifted a fist, held it a moment in front of her face, then jabbed it swiftly into her open mouth and bit down hard on the knuckles. Her shoulders convulsed, but no sound emanated from her. To Blackwell, this display of anguish was much worse than hearing her sob wildly and brokenly.

"I'm sorry, *señora,*" he said again, "but have you thought of the other one who was killed? I come from his house. Do you know what I have seen in his home? I have seen his *mujer,* crying as you cry. I have heard a *niño,* asking why his father doesn't come home. There is much grief, *señora,* because of what happened in these mountains. All the grief is not only in this house."

She took her hand from her mouth and stared at him with a strange intentness as if she were really seeing him for the first time. She began to nod again. "Yes. You are right. I have never thought of the other one. I did not know he had a wife and child. Oh, I am selfish, *señor,* I am selfish."

"Do you still wish me to go?" asked Blackwell. "Or will you speak with me?"

She drew a deep breath. She was making an obvious effort at control. "Speak," she said.

"I am only seeking the truth, *señora,*" Blackwell began earnestly. "I know what they say about your son. I can tell you that I do not know whether to believe or disbelieve. But my employer, *Señor* Jesse Gray, had eight thousand dollars on him when he was killed. I am seeking to recover that money for his wife and his son. Do you understand? I do not want to hurt anyone. But I want to know what happened to that money. I want to know who took it. Was it your son, *señora?*"

The woman's face contorted with grief and indignation. "Are you, too, calling my boy a thief? My Miguelito never stole so much as a raisin from anyone. My Miguelito was a good, honest boy."

"Are you sure of that, *señora?*" asked Blackwell, hating himself, but proceeding grimly, doggedly. "Would it have been possible for your son to have stolen that money without your knowledge?"

"Never," she cried, shaking her head violently, "never! My son was no thief. Why was he not given a trial? Why was he not given a chance to defend himself? Why was he shot down without mercy?"

"I am trying to find out about the money," Blackwell said patiently. "If your son did not have it, then someone else has it."

"My son was no thief," she insisted. "My Miguelito was no murderer. Those are all lies. He was accused of being a thief and a murderer to provide an excuse for killing him.

Others coveted our land. Because my Miguelito would not yield, he was branded a thief and a murderer, and then he was killed so his land could be taken by those who coveted it."

"There was a witness who saw your son take the money from the *Señor* Gray," said Blackwell quietly.

"No!" the woman shouted. "That man is a lying *gringo* pig! My son did not steal that money! My son did not kill!" She began to sob now, her face in her hands. "Go away. Leave me alone with my sorrow. Go. Go!"

"Yes, *gringo* pig, why don't you go?"

Blackwell whirled, his hand stabbing for the handle of his .44. His fingers found the grip, closed tightly about it, then froze like that. He stood staring into the muzzle of the ornate .45 that gaped at him.

The man stood tensely, his immense shoulders filling the doorway. He was the biggest Mexican Blackwell had ever seen. The fellow stood all of six feet three, and he must have weighed two hundred fifty. In passing through the door, his high-peaked sombrero had been knocked from his head, and the hat now hung from its chin thongs down the big man's back.

There was a sick feeling in Blackwell's stomach as he released his grip on his gun and carefully held his hand away from the gun handle. Hostility and hatred flared lucently in the big Mexican's narrowed, pouchy eyes. He said: "Will you leave us, *Tía* Josefa?"

The woman was staring at the big man with wide, wondering eyes. "Josélito," she whispered.

The Mexican never took his glance from Blackwell. "Did you hear me, *Tía* Josefa? I wish to be alone with this *gringo* pig."

"What are you going to do?"

"I am going to break him in two," snarled Josélito.

"No," said the woman, getting to her feet and going up to the big man. For an instant she was in the line of fire, but before Blackwell could do anything, Josélito struck out with an arm, knocking the woman aside. "No," she said again, clutching at Josélito's sleeve. "You do not know everything. This one, he isn't. . . ."

"I saw his horse, *Tía* Josefa," the Mexican growled in his deep, rumbling voice. "I know enough to make me break this *chingando cabrón* in two! Go now, *Tía!* Instantly!"

Eyes never wavering from Blackwell, Josélito reached out and gave the old woman a push. She uttered a small, forlorn wail, buried her face in her apron, and ran, sobbing, out of the hut. With his heel, Josélito kicked the door shut. Then, reaching behind him, he pushed the bolt home.

"Turn around," he said to Blackwell.

Blackwell spread his hands and tried to put on a friendly appeasing smile. "You have me all wrong, *amigo*."

"I told you to turn around, pig."

Blackwell complied. He heard the other approach swiftly. Then the weight of Blackwell's holster eased as his .44 was lifted. Slowly Blackwell turned to face Josélito once more.

"I can explain everything," said Blackwell. "Why don't you get the *Señora* Gómez back in here? She will back up everything I say."

Josélito's face twisted. "I know enough. I know what happened to Miguel Gómez, and I know who was responsible for it. I have seen the brand on your horse, *gringo* pig. Miguel was like a brother to me."

"Mine isn't the only horse with that brand!" Blackwell cried. "Damn you, listen to me. I don't like any more than you what happened to Gómez. But it wasn't my fault. I only came into the Granadas a few days ago, and Gómez was killed over two months ago. How can you tie me in with that?"

"Lies," snarled Josélito. "Dirty, stinking, *gringo* lies. You are afraid to die, and so you would lie your way into hell in an effort to escape death."

"Listen!" cried Blackwell. "Dammit, listen to me!" Then, sickeningly, he realized the futility of argument. He could shout and rail and rant, but he could not hope to convince the Mexican. Josélito now tossed Blackwell's Colt into a corner of the hut, and then holstered his own ornate .45.

"I could shoot you," he said, "but that would be too quick and easy a way for you to die. I could use a knife on you. I could make you scream and shriek with my *cuchillo,* but it would not satisfy me to kill you in that manner. I want the exquisite pleasure of crushing out your life with my bare hands. I am going to break you in two, *gringo* pig. Miguel was like a brother to me!"

Blackwell opened his mouth to try one last argument, but he closed it without uttering a word. Grimly he watched Josélito move in on him.

The Mexican's immense head ducked down, his shoulders hunched. His huge arms spread out widely in a hungry, eager embrace and the long, thick fingers flexed. His chest swelled with a tremendous breath that popped two buttons open on his cotton shirt. Those huge hands with the writhing fingers lifted slightly.

Blackwell stepped quickly to one side, seeking to evade the eager reach of those hands, but Josélito moved, also, with the swiftness of a cat. His left hand, clutching for Blackwell's throat, missed its mark as Blackwell twisted but still caught hold of the neck of Blackwell's shirt. Blackwell gave a hard jerk and the shirt ripped and he was free. With a savage oath, Josélito flung the piece of cloth from his hand.

Blackwell was brought up against the wall, already breathing hard. There was a tiny window beside him, and with a little effort he could wriggle through the aperture, but he could not hope to accomplish this before Josélito grabbed him. So Blackwell dismissed the window from his mind.

Josélito crouched again. Those arms spread out once more.

The Mexican was wide open for two swift blows in the face, Blackwell thought, but, if he stepped in to hit Josélito, then he would be within range of those encircling arms. He ducked a little, started a swing at Josélito's jaw. As the Mexican straightened swiftly with a cry of triumph and started to close his arms, Blackwell lunged and spun and got past.

Blackwell leaped for the door. He got one hand on the bolt, and then he felt a brutal clutch on his shoulder. A roar ripped out of Josélito. Blackwell felt himself being turned against his will, and then he was hurtling backward. He had a brief, blurred vision of Josélito's rage-contorted features, and then he slammed against the wall. The force of it stunned Blackwell.

Josélito's hands were almost upon him before his body began to respond again to the commands of his mind. With his back to the wall, he threw up a leg to kick at Josélito's belly. Growling with rage, the Mexican chopped down with his fist, slamming Blackwell's boot aside, and drove in.

Blackwell could smell the sweat of the big man's body and the stench of pepper and sour wine on his breath. He struck out with all his might at Josélito's face. The blow slammed into Josélito's cheek and turned his head half around, but it did not deter the Mexican. He grunted with pain and started forward again.

Again Blackwell struck at Josélito's face. It was like pounding a fist against a stone wall. The blow had no effect on the big man. His arms circled Blackwell's body and began to squeeze. At this last instant, before he would be crushed against the Mexican's chest, Blackwell remembered the knife haft he had seen sticking out of Josélito's sash. Blackwell got his hand there just as the big man hugged him tightly. With a powerful jerk, Blackwell drew the knife.

Josélito felt the move. A howl of wrath burst out of him. His arms released their hold on Blackwell. A massive fist rose swiftly and smashed against the back of Blackwell's neck. He had the knife out and poised for a stab at the Mexican, but the blow sent Blackwell sprawling, his body all numb. The knife flew from his fingers. Before he could snatch it up again, Josélito had kicked the blade out of reach.

Blackwell rose to his feet as fast as he could, but, before he could set himself, Josélito was upon him again. Blackwell jabbed at the man's belly, but Josélito did not even grunt. Again his tremendous arms clutched Blackwell and hugged him with brutish fury. Now Blackwell was gripped tightly and securely.

He tried jabbing at Josélito's legs with his spurs, but, held as he was, Blackwell could not accomplish this. He began to claw at Josélito's face and eyes. The Mexican only buried his chin down against Blackwell's shoulders and squeezed tighter.

"I will crush the breath out of you," Josélito growled savagely. "I will break you in two."

Blackwell closed both fists in Josélito's hair, but he lacked the strength to pull hard enough to cause the big man any hurt. The world began to weave and spin and heave convulsively. Bright flashes of pain seared his eyeballs. The agony kept growing in his chest, and then he felt his grip on consciousness start to slip.

At this moment Blackwell thought he heard someone shouting and screaming in a shrill voice, but he could not be sure. There was a great roaring in his ears. He thought he heard gunshots, and then the crushing grip on him was loosened. He found himself on the floor with the world still reeling and pin-wheeling, agony still racking his body.

He drew great, rasping breaths into his burning lungs. The world steadied, and his eyes cleared and finally he could see. Josélito stood there, thoroughly cowed, fingering the lobe of an ear that a bullet had slashed. Someone was vehemently denouncing him from the window. Blackwell turned his glance that way. Standing outside the window, pistol thrust through the aperture and aimed at Josélito, was the woman of the inn of San Felipe.

Chapter Five

When he had recovered sufficiently, Blackwell went outside. Josélito was standing over by his horse, a huge hammer-headed roan. The Mexican seemed chagrined, but the look he threw at Blackwell was full of hostility.

Blackwell paused just outside the door and straightened and stretched himself, slowly and carefully, shutting his eyes to the pain that this movement brought him. He had retrieved his .44 from where Josélito had thrown it, and now Blackwell checked the loads in the weapon.

The woman who had rescued Blackwell helped *Señora* Gómez into the hut. Blackwell could hear her low voice soothing the quietly sobbing old woman. After a while, she appeared.

Blackwell looked at her and said: "Thanks."

There was no hint of friendliness about her. She still wore the brown and white calfskin vest and the worn *chivarras* of that night in San Felipe, and her manner was just as chilled and inimical.

"You've caused enough trouble here, Blackwell," she said. "Why don't you go?"

This constant antagonism and mistrust he had encountered since coming into the Granadas made Blackwell irritable and mean. If only he had met one friendly, helpful person, he could have overlooked the rest. His mouth tightened stubbornly.

"I'm only going about my business," he said evenly. "What's wrong with that?"

The girl raised a hand and pointed at the house. "Do you have to pick on a helpless old woman?" she asked.

"I wasn't picking on anybody!" Blackwell flared, rubbing his sore wrist. "If somebody would only tell me what I want to know, instead of throwing dust all over the trail, I wouldn't bother anybody like *Señora* Gómez."

The girl's eyes narrowed slightly. "What is it that you want to know?"

"What happened to the eight thousand dollars Jesse Gray had on him when he was robbed and killed?"

"Why don't you ask Chandler and Hogarth and young Sheppard?"

"I haven't seen Chandler yet," said Blackwell, "but Hogarth and Sheppard claim Mike Gómez had the money. They say he hid it before he was killed."

Josélito emitted a growl of rage, but at a signal from the girl he subsided. The girl's lips pinched with anger. "So you believe it of Mike, too. Why?"

"I didn't say I believe it," said Blackwell. "Like I just told you, I'm just trying to find out what really happened. I want to recover that money. I want to find Chandler. Do you know where he is?"

"Chandler is a dirty liar," said the girl with vehemence. "He wouldn't tell anybody the truth. Not even you."

"I'll take the chance," said Blackwell. "Where can I find him?"

The girl smiled without mirth. It reminded Blackwell of the snarling grimace of a panther. "I just wish I knew. You can bet your life he wouldn't hang out anywhere I could find him. That's all I'm living for, Blackwell . . . to find Chandler and kill him!"

The relentless hatred in her tone turned Blackwell cold. He glanced from the girl to where Josélito stood, still glowering. "Is that why he tried to kill me? Did he think I was Chandler?"

"That's right," said the girl. "Josélito just came from Mexico. He knew what had happened to Mike. He knew about Chandler and the Bar G Bar brand on his horse. So he figured you were Chandler. You're lucky I showed up, Blackwell."

"I already thanked you," said Blackwell.

"That's right, you have," the girl said coldly. "So why don't you get on your horse and leave?"

Blackwell swallowed his resentment. "What is your name?" he asked.

"That is of no interest whatever to you," she answered stiffly.

"You had better go, *yanqui,*" said Josélito, speaking for the first time.

Blackwell turned and faced the Mexican. Josélito was idly fingering the haft of his knife. Rebellion rose in Blackwell, but he let it ride. Going over to his bay, he swung up in the kack. He turned his head to look at the girl, but she had gone back in the house. So Blackwell stared down at Josélito.

"Maybe we'll meet again, *amigo,*" Blackwell said tightly. "I'll be ready for you if that time ever comes."

"Splendid, *yanqui,*" murmured Josélito. "You will not find me reluctant."

To see if he was being followed, Blackwell doubled back. He had progressed several miles up the floor of this cañon, and now he sent the bay up one of the high, sloping walls of this immense gash in the Granadas and then turned the horse in the direction from which he had come, all the while studying the slope and the floor of the cañon before him.

Manzanita and sage grew on the slanting walls, but the floor of the cañon was barren. Overhead, the sun beat down out of the brazen sky. The land seemed desolate and empty, and Blackwell was inclined to go along with this impression until he spied the small movement below him.

The man was perhaps a hundred feet down the slope from Blackwell. He crouched behind a thorny manzanita, utterly unaware that he was being observed. The man's attention was riveted on something down on the cañon floor.

Blackwell had no idea who the man was. At first glance he thought it might be Josélito, for the fellow was wearing a high-peaked sombrero, but he lacked the Mexican's immense size. Whoever the man might be, he boded no good for whomever he was watching at the bottom of the cañon. The sun glittered on the rifle in the fellow's hands.

Blackwell crouched there, undecided. He supposed this was none of his business. If he had not doubled back, he would not have run into this, and he was tempted to mount his bay again and get out of there as quietly and unobtrusively as he could.

Then a rider came into view, proceeding up the cañon in the direction that Blackwell had taken. The man hidden on the slope tensed, and Blackwell saw him start to edge the barrel of the rifle around one side of the thicket. Blackwell took another look at the rider on the cañon floor for whom this bushwhack was intended, and this time recognized the horseman. It was Josélito.

The first thing that came into Blackwell's mind was the recollection of how close he had come to being crushed to death in Josélito's powerful clutch. Blackwell experienced an instant of vile joy. This was all that Josélito deserved. Let him be killed. There would be no tears shed for him by Blackwell.

The man behind the manzanita bush wriggled his body into a more comfortable position and began to sight down the barrel of the rifle.

Sweat popped out on Blackwell's forehead. He was being

a party to a cowardly murder, his mind told him. He tried not to heed this thought. He tried to kneel there and watch with pleasure in his heart. But he could not do it.

No matter how much he disliked Josélito, Blackwell had to admit that the Mexican had acted on a mistaken premise. Josélito was cruel and he was brutal, but he did not strike Blackwell as a man who would take advantage of another just because his back was turned. Josélito deserved a better way to die.

Blackwell threw the Winchester to his shoulder and snapped off a shot. The slug screamed above the head of the man behind the manzanita. The fellow shouted in alarm, and then he was rolling over on his back and aiming the rifle up the slope at Blackwell.

Blackwell fired again, once more throwing the slug a little high by way of warning, but the man down below was having none of this. His rifle blasted, and the bullet slammed the hat from Blackwell's head.

Blackwell's teeth gritted. He lowered his sights a little, caught the fellow's chest in them, and fired. The man seemed to heave convulsively up off the ground as the slug tore into him. He started to scream, but it did not last long. The shriek choked off abruptly. He thrashed his arms a little, and then he lay still.

Blackwell glanced down below at the cañon floor and saw that Josélito had taken cover. Now Blackwell began edging down the slope toward the man he had killed. Josélito had heard the fellow's dying scream, and, when he saw Blackwell working down toward the spot, he came out into the open and mounted his roan again.

The dead man lay with his head pointing down the slope, his arms thrown out wide, one knee pulled up in a last spasm of agony. His face was turned to one side, and the whites of his eyes showed, and a gush of blood had burst out of his mouth to form a small, carmine pool on the ground.

Blackwell waited, standing over the dead man, for Josélito to come up the slope. The Mexican's eyes were narrowed warily, his big teeth bared in a silent, ferine snarl. He stepped down from the saddle, gave a look at the dead man, then kicked the corpse viciously in the side and growled an obscene oath.

"You saved my life, *yanqui,*" he said.

"I'm not proud of it," said Blackwell, his voice tight.

"Why did you do it?"

"I wouldn't let even a dog be shot from behind," said Blackwell. He turned and started up the slope.

"Amigo," said Josélito.

Blackwell heard him come up the slope. Fury blazed across Blackwell's mind. He whirled, Winchester leveled, and Josélito brought up sharply, his massive belly scant inches from the muzzle of the rifle.

"Will you stop following me?" shouted Blackwell. "Or do you want me to give it to you here and now?"

Josélito spread his hands. A hurt look came over his features. *"Amigo,"* he said again.

Blackwell was trembling with anger. He kept remembering how close he had been to death because of this man, and now he had just saved the fellow's life.

"What are you doing here?" Blackwell shouted. "You're following me, aren't you? Do you want to try to kill me again? I'll kill you first!"

"Amigo," said Josélito for a third time. He was pleading. "Listen to me. Listen to me in the way I never listened to you. Josélito is your friend. Believe me. I wish to help you. I wouldn't listen to you, and I almost killed you because of it. Would you want to do the same thing, *amigo?* Because I have

no control over my temper, because I am a fool, must you be one, too?"

The withering anger began to ebb in Blackwell. He lowered the rifle. He would not look at Josélito.

"You were following me," said Blackwell sullenly. "Why?"

"You are looking for that pig, Chandler. I wish to find him, too. I was thinking, perhaps if I followed you, *amigo,* you would lead me to him."

"I'm no *amigo* of yours."

Josélito gestured helplessly again with his hands and sighed. "You will need a friend for what you are trying to do here in the Granadas. You have no idea what you are getting into, Blackwell. After you left us, I was told why you had come here. I sympathize with your purpose, *amigo,* and I wish to help you. Selfishly, perhaps, because at the same time I will be serving my own ends."

"What's your stake in this?" asked Blackwell.

"Miguel Gómez was a cousin of mine, how many times removed I have no idea, but he was still a cousin of Josélito. I used to come up here in the Granadas and stay with Miguel when the . . . ah . . . climate of Mexico became disagreeable with me. I was very fond of the boy. He was no thief and much less a murderer." Josélito's voice took on that ugly growl. "When I find Chandler, I will break him in two!"

Blackwell pointed with his rifle at the dead man. "Where does he come into this?"

Josélito shrugged. "He has nothing to do with you or with Miguel Gómez. He is, shall we say, a result of politics? There are those in Mexico who call me a bandit and those who call me a revolutionist. There is a price upon my head and many who would like to collect it." He turned and directed a malevolent look down the slope at the dead man. "This is the first time their agents have followed me across the border. I had not thought they wanted me so badly." He faced Blackwell again and flashed a sudden smile. "Now do you understand, *amigo,* why the climate of Mexico is so hot for me?"

Blackwell said quietly: "Would you stop following me while I look for Chandler? As a favor to me, Josélito?"

The big man took his arm away from Blackwell and dropped back a step. "I only want to help," he said in an injured tone. "I want to help you find Chandler."

"Look," said Blackwell, "I want to speak to him. You might lose your head, and I would not want Chandler hurt before he has a chance to talk. I have to find those eight thousand dollars. Do you understand, Josélito?"

"Oh, yes," said Josélito.

"Then you will do nothing until I have a chance to find Chandler and talk to him?"

"Josélito promises."

Chapter Six

Blackwell rode on through the Granadas, skirting the holdings of Lazy S, and passed beyond the vast acreage of this ranch to where the land was divided among smaller outfits. He spent one night at one of these small spreads. The place was owned by a middle-aged bachelor who worked his ranch alone, and he was very happy to have company for the night and turned out to be most garrulous. He told Blackwell that Chandler had been staying with one Fred Crabtree who had a place just half a day's ride away.

In the morning Blackwell went looking for Crabtree. As Blackwell rode on, the mountains grew more desolate and barren. By now, he had seen enough of the Granadas to know that the choicest and lushest graze belonged to Lazy S. The immediate neighbors of Lazy S had fairly good ground, but once beyond them the Granadas were only wasteland.

Yet men had tried their luck in this part of the mountains, too. Blackwell saw the monuments to their failures in a couple of abandoned and broken shacks and in a deserted mine diggings. He began to wonder what a man like Crabtree would be doing in an unpromising and discouraging locale like this. It gave Blackwell a hint as to the kind of man Fred Crabtree must be.

When Blackwell finally arrived at the place, he thought at first glance that it, too, was deserted. The small clapboard house stood at the bottom of a desolate hill covered only by sage and greasewood. There were a couple of cottonwoods growing to one side of the house, and between the trees there was a well, which explained why anyone so much as dared to try residence in this forsaken country.

The first thing that hit him was the reek of the place. It was almost like a blow in the face, stepping into it suddenly from the clean, dry scent of the air outside. Blackwell left the door open, and the rush of fresh air into the one room alleviated the smell a little.

The sound of snoring directed Blackwell's attention, and he saw a man sleeping on the bunk in one corner of the room. Blackwell walked over to the bunk, trying not to heed the stink but having very little luck. A man would have to be dead not to mind this stench.

The fellow lay flat on his back with all his clothes on. His mouth was very wide as if he could not breathe at all through his nose, and the breath kept rattling and gurgling and snorting deeply in his throat. He had been drinking in bed when he had fallen asleep for his left hand still grasped a bottle, but so limp was his hold that the bottle had tipped over and most of whatever had been in it had been soaked up by the dirty, greasy blanket on which the fellow was lying.

He had on a worn and soiled pair of white cotton trousers supported by a brace of red galluses. He was wearing no shirt. Beneath the galluses was a long-sleeved, cotton undershirt, which also was very dirty. Looking at the man's face and hands, Blackwell doubted if the fellow had washed within the last month.

Blackwell started shaking the shoulder. "You Fred Crabtree?" he asked.

The man recovered enough to reach up with his right hand and push Blackwell's fingers off his shoulder. The fellow's eyes opened to tiny slits.

"Go away," he groaned. "There's nobody here."

"Are you Crabtree?" asked Blackwell.

Those slitted eyes stared anguishedly at Blackwell a while. Then the man said: "I don't know you. If you want something, help yourself to it. I'm awful tired. I got to sleep."

"I want to talk to you, Crabtree," said Blackwell. "I want to ask you about Luke Chandler."

Crabtree raised a hand and dropped the palm over his aching eyes. He groaned once and then lay there, working his mouth dryly. He made no effort to speak.

Blackwell motioned to Crabtree to sit up on his bunk. The man complied. He sat there, staring at Blackwell out of pink-veined, luminous, suffering eyes. Crabtree appeared to be in his forties. He was small and withered, his chest curved inward and at the bottom came out to form a small, round potbelly. He had sandy hair that was very thin at the top.

Blackwell said: "I've been told that Luke Chandler has been staying here with you."

"I don't know nothing."

"Do you want me to get tough with you, Crabtree?"

The man licked his lips nervously. He darted a look at the bottle that Blackwell now held in his hand.

"Could I have a little drink?" whined Crabtree. He rubbed his chest. "The pain in my chest is something awful now. Just a little nip? Please?"

"All right," said Blackwell reluctantly. He handed the bottle over. "But you better tell me what I want to know."

Crabtree grabbed the bottle with both hands. He shook violently as he brought it up, but, once he had it in his mouth and began swallowing, his trembling quickly ceased.

Blackwell had to take the bottle away from him. "Well, what do you know about Chandler?"

Crabtree hung his head. "I never heard of the *hombre,*" he said sullenly.

Anger writhed in Blackwell's brain. He glanced around the dirty, stinking room and saw the shelf on the wall, the shelf with a row of six whisky bottles on it. Blackwell drew his gun.

Even with his eyes closed, Crabtree sensed the move. His head flung up. "What you gonna do?" he cried.

"Just this," said Blackwell. He aimed the Colt carefully and fired. The house seemed to shake with the roar of the .44. One of the whisky bottles shattered into shards. The smell of the spilled whisky began to mingle with the other odors of the place. Blackwell thought the addition improved the aroma.

"O-oh," moaned Crabtree, putting his face in his hands. He began to shake all over.

"Well, Crabtree?"

When the man did not reply, Blackwell lifted his .44 and aimed again. At the sound of the second shot and the shatter of breaking glass, Crabtree jerked convulsively, lifting up off the edge of the bunk, then came down hard. Horror-stricken, he gazed at the two broken whisky bottles and at the liquor dripping with gentle *plops* on the floor.

Blackwell said: "You're quite a way from town, Crabtree. I would say you'd have to go almost two days, at least, before you could get to where you could buy some more liquor. Do you think you could hold out that long without a little nip?" He raised the gun quickly and fired again. Now there were only three bottles left.

Crabtree jumped to his feet. "Please," he sobbed, dropping to his knees and clutching at Blackwell's chaps. "Please don't. I'm a sick man. I'd die without my whisky. I couldn't stand the pain in my chest without my medicine."

Blackwell fired again. "You've got two bottles left," he said coldly.

Crabtree groveled. He pawed at Blackwell's chaps. "All right," he sobbed. "All right, I'll tell you."

"Why does Chandler come here at all?" asked Blackwell.

"He's a sick man, too," whined Crabtree. "He buys the liquor, and then he comes here, and we drink."

"The Luke Chandler I know isn't a drinking man," said Blackwell.

"He's sick now. That's why he drinks."

"You said you were not supposed to tell me anything. Who told you not to?"

Crabtree moaned and started shaking his head. "I didn't know what I was saying. It's just something that came out of me. I'm all mixed up inside. I'm a sick man."

"Where is Chandler?"

"I don't know."

Blackwell felt disgust and loathing as he looked down at the craven Crabtree. "Get up off the floor," said Blackwell, "and then tell me where I can find Chandler."

Crabtree rose hesitantly to his feet. He sniffled and kept his eyes turned down. "I don't know," he said again.

Blackwell's lips tightened. He put his hand on the butt of his Colt. "Do you want me to break another bottle?"

"Oh, no!" cried Crabtree, lifting beseeching hands. "Won't you believe me when I tell you I don't know? Chandler was here yesterday, and then he went to see somebody. He always does that. He rides off to see somebody, but he never tells me who it is or where he goes. That is God's truth. I swear it."

"Why should I believe you?" Blackwell asked coldly.

"This time it's the truth. It's God's truth. I swear it. I swear it!"

"Should I break another bottle?"

"What are you, Blackwell, a temperance worker or something?" asked someone behind Blackwell.

He spun on his heel, drawing his .44, and then he froze with the weapon in his hand, feeling foolish over what he had done. Facing him, one hand propped indolently against the doorframe, was the blonde woman named Angel Dawson.

Chapter Seven

She stood there, watching him with a faint amusement in her strange gray eyes. Blackwell felt the blood rush to his face, and he hurriedly holstered his .44, experiencing more and more discomfort under the persistence of that cool, bemused stare.

She said: "Have you taken it upon yourself to go around destroying the evil menace of demon rum, Blackwell? Are you starting out to break every liquor bottle you see?"

She was dressed the same as when Blackwell had seen her that other time in War Feather. A black and red flannel shirt, a buckskin divided riding skirt, but now she wore a cream-colored Stetson set at a jaunty angle on her yellow hair. Another addition was the shell belt strapped about her slim waist, with the holstered .44, butt pointing forward on her left hip.

Crabtree had lost his fear. He became indignant. "Look what he did, Angel!" Crabtree cried. "Just look what he did. He came in my home bold as you please and started shooting my bottles to pieces!"

"You'll get some more medicine," said the woman. "They make it a little bit faster than you can drink it." She wrinkled her nose and said to Blackwell: "Do you like that smell? Or would you just as soon step outside with me?" Without waiting for Blackwell's answer, she turned and walked away.

Blackwell glanced at Crabtree. The man had turned from his liquor shelf and had picked up the part-emptied bottle that Blackwell had set down on the table. Now Crabtree put the bottle to his mouth and began to swallow noisily and happily. Blackwell went outside.

The woman was standing in the shade of a cottonwood tree. She had taken off her hat and was fanning her face with it. Blackwell felt something stir in him. She was a very desirable woman.

A handsome Arabian was standing beside Blackwell's bay. The saddle on the Arabian had a lot of silverwork on it and so did the bridle. Blackwell's breath was almost taken away by the sleek beauty of the woman's horse.

The woman said: "Did you really have to be so rough on poor Fred? He's quite harmless."

To hide the discomfiture that still existed in him, Blackwell growled: "I was trying to find out something."

"Why don't you ask me?" said the woman. "You don't have to bust any whisky bottles with me." She seemed to be secretly laughing at him.

Blackwell flushed again. He began to get angry with this woman's easy, jibing way. He said: "Do you know Luke Chandler?"

"I've seen him around."

"Do you know where he is?"

The woman stopped fanning her face. She placed the hat back on her head and carefully adjusted the Stetson at a cocky angle. Then she tightened the thongs under her chin. "That would be hard to say," she declared at last. "He keeps moving around pretty much."

"How come?" asked Blackwell.

"Chandler is scared."

"Scared of what?"

The woman shrugged. "He's got good reason for being scared. The Mexicans up around San Felipe are pretty much worked up about the killing of Mike Gómez. They blame Chandler for it because Chandler identified Gómez as the bandit who robbed and killed this Jesse Gray. So Chandler keeps moving around, just so he won't run into any of these pals of Gómez."

Blackwell's eyes narrowed a little. "You seem to know pretty much about this thing," he observed quietly.

"Not particularly," she said. "I know all the talk that's gone around about it, that's all. Practically everyone in the Granadas knows as much as I do."

Blackwell hitched a thumb at the horse. "Has Chandler been staying here?"

"Off and on."

"Is he drinking heavily?"

"That's right. He seemed pretty upset over the death of Gray. I imagine they were pretty good friends."

Blackwell said slowly: "You know a lot about Luke Chandler. How well are you acquainted with him?"

"Like I said, I've seen Chandler around. I know who he is, but that's about all. I've told you all I know, Blackwell."

"Thanks," said Blackwell. He turned to his bay and tightened the cinch.

The woman asked: "Where are you going now?"

"I'm going to keep on looking for Chandler," he told her.

"Do you know where to look?"

"No. But I'll look anyway."

She hitched a thumb in her shell belt and drummed the fingers of that hand against the leather. "You are stubborn," she sad softly, almost as if to herself. Then she smiled suddenly at him, her teeth flashing. "Mind if I ride along with you? I'm anxious to get away from here. This place gives me the creeps."

She stepped over to her Arabian, tightened the cinch, and then swung gracefully up into the saddle. She looked down, brows lifting, at Blackwell, who still stood, undecided, on the ground.

"Are we going to wait all day, Blackwell?" she asked.

He grunted annoyedly. He did not like what she was stirring inside him, for he wanted nothing to interfere with his job, but he was helpless against the sensation. He mounted the bay. "All right," he said roughly. "Let's go."

Late that afternoon they came to a creek, an unexpected benison in this parched stretch of the Granadas. Aspens grew on both sides of the creek. This was high country here. The air was thin and cold.

The girl dismounted from her Arabian, and, dropping on her stomach on the edge of the creek, she put her mouth in the water and drank, not far from where the Arabian was thirstily drinking. Blackwell, also, satisfied his thirst, and, when he was done, he saw that Angel Dawson was finished, too. She sighed with pleasure and wiped her mouth with the back of her hand.

Then she walked slowly over to him, her head cocked a little to one side, her hands clasped behind her back. As she moved, he could see the stir of her breath under the black and red flannel shirt.

The joshing easiness seemed gone from her manner. She looked very sober and earnest. She came to a halt not five feet from him and said: "Look, Blackwell"—holding out a hand with the palm up in a gesture of exasperation—"this thing is finished, it's done with. Why do you want to keep tampering with it? Why don't you let the whole thing die down? It would be best for everybody."

"I'll let it rest," said Blackwell, "as soon as I find that eight thousand dollars."

"You'll never find it," said Angel Dawson.

"Why won't I?"

"Because Mike Gómez hid the money and he's dead and

your chances of finding where Gómez cached the money aren't worth a hoot in hell."

"How do you know Gómez had the money? How do you know he buried it?"

"Didn't Chandler say so?"

"Did he?" asked Blackwell. "I never heard Chandler say so. By now he should know I'm in the Granadas. Everyone else seems to know who I am and why I'm here. Why does Chandler keep running from me?"

"Don't you believe Gómez robbed and killed Gray?"

"Maybe Gómez did," said Blackwell, "but I haven't been convinced yet."

"Have you been talking to Margarita Luz?"

"Margarita Luz? Who is she?"

"A friend of Gómez. Has she turned your head from the truth, Blackwell?"

Blackwell inhaled a deep breath. "Is that all there is to it?" he asked. "Because Gómez was a Mexican, he was no good. Because his friends are, they're all liars."

She lifted her hands exasperatedly. Her voice rose. "But there was a witness to everything. He saw Gómez rob and kill Gray. What more do you want?"

"I want the eight thousand dollars."

"Oh, hell, Blackwell," she said in disgust. "Stop singing the same song over and over." She came ahead and put a hand on his sleeve. She was very close now. The odor of lilacs was strong in his nostrils. "Can't you understand yet why Chandler doesn't want to see you? He's broken up about the whole thing."

"There's someone else broken up," said Blackwell grimly. "There's Missus Gray and her son."

The girl's head dropped. The fire went abruptly out of her, and Blackwell saw her bite her lip. "There are certain things that can't be helped, Blackwell. I'm sorry about it. But it can't be helped."

"I'm sorry, too," he said, "but I'm going to do something about it. I'm not going to stand around and say it's too bad and then forget about it. I can't forget about it!" he shouted. He grasped the girl's arm with such strength that she winced. "Missus Gray is my sister, and little Davey Gray is my nephew. Neither you nor that dude, Sheppard, nor Hogarth are keeping me from Chandler and that money!"

"Bobby Sheppard?" asked the girl, her eyes wide with surprise.

"Yes, young Sheppard," said Blackwell. "He sent you after me, didn't he? Him and Hogarth. They're the ones who tipped off Chandler about me. They're the ones keeping Chandler from me. They sent you to get me to lay off because they've got the eight thousand dollars!"

"Do you really believe that someone sent me to you?"

"I do."

"Couldn't I have come to you of my own free will?"

"Why?"

She reached up and caught the flaps of his jumper. Her eyes lidded in a half-shy, half-bold manner. Her voice became low and throaty and softly provocative. "Why?" she asked. "I'm hard-boiled, and I never believed in love, but that was before I saw you. I know, you're thinking of Bobby Sheppard and what you've probably heard about me being his girl. Well," she said, taking a deep breath "I run around with Bobby. He's got money, and he buys me nice things, and I've always been selfish because I never really loved a man. I see nothing wrong in that. Bobby knows I don't love him. If he wants to waste his time and money on me, that's his business."

Her hands gripped the flaps of Blackwell's jumper so

tightly that the knuckles showed white. She edged in closer to him. Blackwell was very conscious of her nearness, of her warmth, of her fragrance and desirability.

"What I'm going to tell you, Blackwell," she went on, "is something no woman should tell a man unless he's told her first. But you're suspicious of me, you doubt me, so I'll tell you. It was you for me the minute I laid eyes on you. Don't you remember how I stared at you? Or didn't you notice? It was then that I knew. Only you, and no one else."

She edged still closer. He could feel the light and firm pressure of her breasts through his shirt. A cloying ache filled Blackwell's throat.

"Don't you understand, yet, why I've talked to you the way I have? I'm scared for you, Blackwell," she said huskily, a catch in her voice. "I'm scared of what might happen to you. You keep driving ahead stubbornly, blindly, antagonizing everyone you meet. One of these days you're going to insult someone a little too much. You're going to get yourself killed if you don't stop. I'm afraid that someday I'll come riding into the Granadas and find your dead body."

He could feel the desire grow in him. He knew what it was that had troubled him every time he had looked at Angel Dawson. It was deep and poignant in his heart because those uncertainties still lived in him, he still could not shake the distrust, no matter what his heart told him.

"I can't give it up, Angel," he said thickly. "I'm not built that way. I can't give it up."

"Please, Blackwell," she begged. "What would I do if anything happened to you? I'd never get over it. I love you, Blackwell."

"Angel," he began, and then he could say no more. He knew how he felt but he could not put it into words. The emotion was too overwhelming for him.

"Don't you care at all for me?" asked the girl, pressing hard against him, her mouth lifting.

Blackwell realized that he could no longer hold back. It was her hot pressure against him, his yearning for her that must have been borne in him the first instant he had seen her. Suddenly all the mistrust was gone, all the doubts were dead. He felt a great rush of passion through him.

"Angel," he said thickly. "Angel." He bent his head, mouth seeking hers. She came to him fervidly and eagerly.

Chapter Eight

Blackwell returned to War Feather. His failure to find anything in the Granadas had, for the moment, discouraged him. He did not expect to find anything in War Feather, either, but it was the only place he could think to go.

He ate supper and then decided to have a few drinks before going to bed. This time he pointedly avoided the Longhorn Saloon. A place called the Silver Saddle attracted him, and he went in.

There was a fair crowd in the place. The kerosene lanterns had been lighted, and their flickering, smoky light illuminated the barroom. The bar was half filled, and at a couple of the tables poker games were in progress. The soft hum of conversation, a laugh now and then, the jingle of spurs, and the muted scrape of boots, all these sounds floated through the place. It made Blackwell feel good.

People came and went. From his position at the end of the bar, Blackwell could see their passing in and out of the batwings. It was thus that he noticed Tex Hogarth enter the place.

Hogarth stopped just inside the batwings and ran his glance over the room. He quickly spotted Blackwell and their eyes locked. Hogarth did not speak immediately. The amusement seemed to grow and swell in his eyes, but there was nothing pleasant in the mirth. Finally Hogarth said: "Why do you keep on telling lies about me and Bobby Sheppard, Blackwell?"

Blackwell felt the wrath begin again in him. Recollection of that other time in the Longhorn kept flashing across his mind. His lips tightened.

"I won't take any rawhiding from you, Hogarth. Even with young Sheppard backing you up. I won't take any rawhiding this time!"

"Who said anything about rawhiding?" Hogarth asked softly. "I just want to know what you've got against me that you have to keep spreading dirty lies about me."

There was now a discreet moving away of all the drinkers from the bar. A silence settled over the place.

"Who's been telling you tales, Hogarth?"

"That doesn't enter into it," said Hogarth. "This is just between you and me. Don't try to bring anybody else into it."

"Not even Bobby Sheppard?"

"Just you and me, Blackwell."

"Where is young Sheppard?"

"Why ask me?" said Hogarth.

"You two *hombres* strike me as being very brave when one of you is in front and the other is behind. Is that why you're talking so big, Hogarth? Is Sheppard somewhere behind me?"

"I don't need Sheppard," said Hogarth, displaying the first sign of anger. "I can handle you alone."

"What makes you think that?" Blackwell asked, taking one step away from the bar. "Because your gun is tied down and mine isn't? Or did someone send you to try to take care of me?"

"No one sent me," snarled Hogarth. His small, cruel mouth was turned down at one end; there no longer was any amusement in his eyes. "You're a dirty, god-damn' liar, Blackwell!"

He was fast. His right hand dipped and in the same instant seemed to have the big Remington out of its holster. Ever since Hogarth had first opened his mouth to speak to him, Blackwell had been ready for this. His own .44 whipped out.

He thumbed off a shot as fast as he could, and at that precise instant it seemed that Hogarth's gun bucked and roared in his hand. A bullet made a vicious, snarling *hiss* past Blackwell's ear. He saw Hogarth stagger, and then heard him grunt in pain. But Hogarth quickly recovered. His .44 was wavering a little, but he steadied it for another try.

Blackwell fired again. This time Hogarth's gun was a definite echo to the roar of Blackwell's weapon. This slug slammed Hogarth halfway around and smashed him up against the bar. The gun dropped from his fingers. Pain lay gray and contorted on his features.

With a slow, deliberate gesture, Hogarth bent down to pick up his gun. But as his fingers found the handle, his knees gave way, and he stayed himself from going flat on his face by planting the palms of his hands against the floor. On hands and knees, he lifted a straining face and glared at Blackwell. Hogarth's fingers again closed about the handle of his Remington.

Blackwell fired again.

Tex Hogarth was dead. . . .

Chapter Nine

Early the next morning, Blackwell rode out of War Feather. He crossed the small stretch of desert, and then began to climb up into the Granadas. He was headed in the direction of San Felipe.

He had slept little the previous night. The killing of Hogarth had upset Blackwell a little, but the principal cause of his unrest had been all those nagging thoughts in his mind. He had gone over the matter time and again. He was convinced that Hogarth had been sent to kill him to keep him from probing deeper into the death of Jesse Gray. Who, Blackwell asked himself until his head began to ache, had sent Hogarth?

Blackwell tried to assemble the facts to see if they would make any sense. Hogarth had worked for Lazy S; he had chummed around with Bobby Sheppard. Had someone on Lazy S sent Hogarth on his mission of death? Blackwell would have ridden out to Lazy S, but, after having killed its ramrod, he felt it would be more prudent if he went at it from another direction.

Again Blackwell's mental peregrinations returned to Luke Chandler. What was the truth about Chandler? Was he a terror-stricken sot, intimidated into keeping out of sight—or was he the mysterious somebody who seemed to be directing everything from some secret hiding place?

Blackwell's thought turned to Angel Dawson. What was her part in this? She, too, had tried to dissuade him. The only connection Blackwell could see for her was through her relationship with Bobby Sheppard, and this in turn brought him back to Lazy S.

For a while, he had also considered the sheriff, Frank Richmond. There was a possibility that the man was involved and using his official capacity to cover up the actual perpetrators of the crime. Richmond ostensibly was lazy and shiftless, but he struck Blackwell as being a shrewd, cunning person.

The only remaining tangent for Blackwell was Mike Gómez. If Gómez were guilty, then that settled the matter. There was no point in any further investigation. But if Gómez had been framed, and by now Blackwell was inclined to believe this, then Blackwell's most favorable course of action would be to find out who would have been most likely to frame the dead man. For this reason, Blackwell rode back into the Granadas, seeking Margarita Luz.

The next morning Blackwell came to the girl's home. Her parents ran a small sheep ranch several miles from San Felipe. They told Blackwell that the girl was out tending the sheep that day. They told him where the flock could be found, and Blackwell thanked them and rode away.

He found the flock grazing in a small mountain meadow. A tiny creek ran along one edge of the meadow, and, when Blackwell rode out from the pines, the girl was watering her pinto in the stream. She turned swiftly as he came up behind her. Her right hand made a pass at the handle of the .41 at her hip.

Margarita Luz was the woman who had rescued him from Josélito.

Blackwell reined in the bay, and then he leaned forward in his kack and folded his forearms across his saddle horn. "Are you always this cordial when someone calls on you?" he asked her as she stood tensely on the ground, staring suspiciously up at him. Her hand still gripped the handle of the .41 at her hip.

With her face turned up like that, the sun fell on it.

Blackwell found himself marveling at the gentle roundness of the cheeks and at the long lashes that half concealed the brown eyes filled with distrust and hostility.

"What do you want?" asked Margarita Luz.

"I'd like to talk with you."

"There's nothing for us to talk about."

"I think there is," said Blackwell. "I'm on your side, Margarita."

She still held onto the grip of the .41. After a while she said: "I don't know what you mean."

"Two nights ago I killed Tex Hogarth," said Blackwell.

He saw the fierce, cruel joy light up her face. Her mouth parted in the first smile Blackwell had ever seen on her, but there was no mirth in it. It was more of a savage grimace than anything else.

"Bueno," she said.

"Now will you talk with me?" asked Blackwell.

She hesitated. He saw the grim pleasure fade from her face, and she began watching him again with that old suspicion. "How do I know you really killed Hogarth?" she asked.

"What do you want me to do? Take his scalp and show it to you?"

The girl flushed. "All right," she said, "you killed Hogarth. Why should that make me trust you?"

"Gómez," said Blackwell.

Her mouth twitched at mention of the name. "That doesn't mean anything," she said stubbornly.

"Can't you see," said Blackwell, spreading his hands in exasperation. "We both want the same thing. I want the eight thousand dollars that was stolen from Gray. You want the name of Gómez cleared and everyone responsible for his death punished. Whoever planned the framing of Gómez has the money. Instead of bucking each other, wouldn't it be better if we worked together?"

"I'm not interested in any money," she said sullenly, but she finally took her hand off her gun. She rubbed the palm against her worn *chivarras*. "I want to get my hands on Chandler. I want him to tell me why he lied about Mike Gómez."

"What about young Sheppard?" asked Blackwell. "Didn't he and Hogarth do the actual killing? From what I've found out, Chandler had no part in the killing. He just identified Gómez as the bandit and murderer. Why haven't you done anything about Sheppard? He shouldn't be hard to find."

"Chandler has to come first. Sheppard is protected by the law. He claims he killed a thief and a murderer. Chandler has to be made to clear Mike Gómez. Then that will make Sheppard a murderer. As for finding him, he is pretty careful to stay out of my way. He is never alone. Once he had Hogarth with him all the time. Now he will get someone else. As for going to Lazy S, I wouldn't get very far. They'd know I was going there for only one thing. No," she said, shaking her head. "It's got to be Chandler first."

Blackwell dismounted. He led the bay to the creek and left the animal drinking.

"I'm trying to find out who really killed Gray and who has Gray's money," he said. "But it seems that whatever I start out on doubles back to where I started. I don't know where to begin any more. So I came to you, Margarita. I thought you might have an idea of how it was."

She shrugged. "I know as much as you do," she said.

"How do you have Chandler figured out?"

"He's the dirty liar who caused the death of Mike Gómez!"

"We'll pass up Chandler, then," said Blackwell. "Why do you think Gómez was framed and who did it?"

"That should be obvious," she said. "It was Lazy S. They

wanted Mike's land. He wouldn't sell, so they decided to get rid of him. You can tell that's how it was by the fact that Lazy S has taken over Mike's ranch."

"Do you think that young Sheppard and Hogarth killed Gray?"

"I do."

"Do you think there was anyone behind Hogarth and Sheppard? Someone who put them up to it?"

She looked keenly at him. "Why would there be? Isn't it enough that Lazy S wanted Mike's place? Sheppard and Hogarth couldn't come right out and kill Mike. They had to have an excuse. So they killed Gray and robbed him, and then got Chandler to claim it was Mike who robbed and killed Gray. Then Sheppard and Hogarth killed Mike and said they did it because he was trying to get away. That's how I've got it figured out."

Blackwell said nothing.

The girl said: "What makes you think there was someone behind Hogarth and Sheppard?"

Blackwell shrugged. "It's just a feeling I have. I can't get over the thought that someone sent Hogarth to kill me. I can't prove it. I just don't think Hogarth came on his own, and I'm pretty sure young Sheppard didn't send him. The impression that I've got of Sheppard is that he's a spoiled brat, a loudmouth. He doesn't have the brains to plan anything like this. He's just being used. There has to be someone behind the thing."

"And you think Chandler might be this someone?"

"He could be, but I doubt it. Like young Sheppard, Chandler hasn't the brains or imagination for a thing like this." He threw a sidelong glance at Margarita Luz. "What kind of a man is the sheriff, Frank Richmond?"

A look of distaste came over the girl's face. "He's just a

lazy politician. Whenever something comes up, Richmond tries to dispose of it in the quickest, most convenient way. That's how it was with Mike. It was very easy to say that Mike robbed and killed Gray and that Mike was killed resisting arrest. According to Richmond, that settled everything."

"Is Richmond an honest man?"

"That all depends on what you mean by honesty," she said. "Oh, I don't think Richmond accepts any outright bribes. He's honest in that respect. And he does try to enforce the law within the limitations of his laziness. But, like I said, he's a politician. Lazy S put him into office. He could never afford to offend Lazy S because that might lose him a lot of votes. So when Hogarth and Sheppard told him about Mike, Richmond went along with their story. It was convenient, it didn't lose him any votes, and, besides, we're only greasers." Her voice was heavy with contempt.

Blackwell said: "Could there be any chance that Richmond is behind all this?"

"That I can't see, Blackwell. Richmond isn't getting anything out of it, unless it's a cut of the money. If he's mixed up in it, he's just one of the hirelings. He's too lazy to be the boss. No, this is all the doing of the Lazy S."

Blackwell could see that he was getting nowhere. It made him feel irritable, but he did not let this feeling show. After all, it wasn't the girl's fault. She was telling him everything she knew.

He tried another tack. "What about this Angel Dawson?"

"Angel Dawson has been running around with Bobby Sheppard ever since she came to the Granadas. She's obviously out to get her hands on Lazy S. Either Sheppard sent her or she came to you of her own accord. After all, she couldn't marry into Lazy S if you should prove Sheppard a murderer and he's either killed or hanged for it."

Blackwell glanced past the girl, and at the edge of the pines he saw the three men. How long they had been standing there, Blackwell had no idea. As he stared, a coldness came into his throat.

Two of the men were pointing rifles at him and the girl.

Chapter Ten

Margarita Luz saw the consternation on Blackwell's face, and she spun around, her hand gesturing to the handle of her gun, but then she saw the three and she froze like that.

When the three saw that neither Blackwell nor the girl was going to draw their weapons, they started coming in. The two with the rifles moved warily, one of them covering the girl, the other Blackwell. The third one walked to one side, careful not to place himself in the line of fire, but definitely preceding the other two. He walked with a swagger that proclaimed him to be the leader, so Blackwell turned his attention principally on this man.

The fellow was a Mexican. He was short and slight, standing perhaps five foot five and weighing no more than one-twenty. He wore a brown *charro* outfit, fancy-stitched short jacket and tight-fitting trousers that were tucked into highly polished boots. He had a yellow sash about his middle and a pearl-handled six-shooter in a holster at his side. A quirt dangled from his left wrist. He wore a high-peaked sombrero that shaded his face. His features were sharp and vain. Piercing black eyes glittered beneath thin, long brows. The nose was thin and aquiline, the mouth was small and prim, yet it still gave an impression of an innate viciousness. A hairline mustache graced the upper lip of the mouth, the points fingered out into sharp tips that curled slightly upward.

The little Mexican came to a halt about ten feet away and motioned with his head to his two men. While one of them covered both Blackwell and the girl, the other came ahead and disarmed them. Blackwell studied these two. They were not impressive in appearance and were clearly the servants of the little man. They both wore white cotton shirts and trousers and huge straw sombreros. Their faces were dull and emotionless.

Blackwell turned his eyes back on the little man and growled: "What the hell is this?"

The little man straightened, drawing himself up perceptibly. His slim shoulders squared, and his chest swelled. He fairly glowed with self-importance and pride. He said: "Permit me to introduce myself." His heels clicked sharply. "I am of the Federal Army of Mexico. *Teniente* Maximo Novarro." He was now speaking to Margarita Luz. "I wish information as to the whereabouts of José Vasquez, also known as Josélito."

Scorn glittered in the girl's eyes. "Why are you looking for him up here? Shouldn't you be looking in Mexico?"

"As you very well know," said Lt. Novarro, "Josélito is no respecter of international boundaries. He comes and goes as he pleases. When he has glutted himself with depredations in our glorious republic, he flees northward into Los Estados Unidos. In the same fashion that Josélito pays no heed to the international marking, I, *Teniente* Maximo Novarro, also pay no heed. As you can plainly see, I am not clothed in the uniform of a lieutenant of the Federal Army of Mexico. My two men, also, are not clothed in their uniforms. We are, to all intents, civilians going about our business . . . which happens to be the apprehension of that butcher and thief, Josélito."

"Then why don't you go out hunting him?" said the girl somewhat sarcastically. "You certainly won't find him by standing around and talking about it."

"Ah?" said Navarro, and Blackwell did not like the sound of it. "Ah? I have a feeling that you are going to be difficult. *¡Bueno!* If that is how you wish it, then that is how it shall be. You shall find me a most accommodating person."

He barked stern orders in that high falsetto of his, and his two men hurried to obey. Blackwell could picture this small martinet shouting commands to a troop of men in that shrill, squeaking voice and the quiet derision these sounds would rouse at first, but, when the men came to know the real Lt. Novarro, they would no longer laugh at the preposterous pitch of his commands. They would lose no time in complying or suffer the consequences.

One of the two soldiers went back into the pines and returned with three horses. Blackwell and the girl were then made to mount their animals after which their wrists were tied and lashed to their saddle horns and feet bound with ropes passed underneath the horses' bellies.

The cavalcade rode off into the Granadas.

They came to a deserted part of the mountains. At the foot of a cliff was a small adobe hut that appeared to have been abandoned for quite some time. The thatched roof had caved in.

Novarro waved a hand. "Behold my headquarters," he said. "Is it not a charming place?" He tittered, and his two men tittered in echo. "However, for my purposes, I could not ask for a more ideal location. One could live here for a year without seeing any one ride past."

He dismounted and motioned to his men. They unbound the feet of Blackwell and the girl, and the two then stepped down to the ground. Standing, their hands still tied, their legs were bound again.

Novarro's eyes lidded a little. The gaiety and jauntiness went out of him; he was chill business now. "I, *Teniente* Maximo Novarro, have ways of finding out things," he said crisply. "I know that you, *Señorita* Margarita Luz, were affianced to Miguel Gómez. It was with Miguel Gómez that

Josélito stayed during his sojourns in this country. Thus, you have come to know José Vasquez, or Josélito, very well. You were seen in the company of Josélito only three days ago." Novarro snapped his fingers. "Come. Where is he?"

The girl shrugged. "How should I know? He comes and goes. I suppose he is somewhere in the Granadas."

"Señorita," Novarro said in his high voice, "do not tempt me to take measures. I, *Teniente* Maximo Novarro, delight in taking measures. However, I shall be patient with you a moment longer. I shall give you another opportunity to comply with my demand. Where is Josélito?"

"Even if I knew, I wouldn't tell you," said the girl.

"So?" said Novarro softly. "So?" He lifted a languid left arm from the wrist of which dangled his quirt. "Behold this whip," he said. "Would you like a taste of it, *Señorita* Luz?"

Novarro said it quietly, in that preposterous child's voice, but still the tone of it struck a chill in Blackwell. "She doesn't know, Novarro," he growled. "Leave her alone, will you?"

"Ah?" Novarro said, turning his head indolently to look at Blackwell. "The *yanqui* has a tongue! Perhaps that tongue can tell *Teniente* Maximo Novarro where to find that murderous wretch and scoundrel, Josélito?"

"Why do you want him?" asked Blackwell.

"Josélito incites rebellion."

"I see," said Blackwell, "and, if you catch him, what will happen?"

Novarro shrugged. "He will undoubtedly be executed."

"Thanks for telling me," said Blackwell dryly.

"I do not like the way you said that," declared Novarro, "but I will overlook it." He walked over and stopped in front of Blackwell. "Would you like a cigarette, *señor?*"

The query surprised Blackwell. He watched the little man dig in a pocket and come out with a pack of brown-paper cigarettes. He selected one and placed it in Blackwell's mouth.

"Am I not good to you?" asked Novarro. "Have I not given you a cigarette to smoke? Am I not kind?"

"Sure," Blackwell said again, finding it difficult to keep the sarcasm out of his tone. However, it went unnoticed by Novarro.

"¡Bueno!" he exclaimed, throwing up his hands in delight and smiling broadly. "Then we are friends?"

"Sure," said Blackwell. "We're regular pals."

Again Novarro missed the sarcasm, or, if he noticed it, he chose to ignore it. He said: "Now that we are friends, there is no reason for one to keep secrets from the other, is there? Very well. Do you know where I could find this Josélito?"

"I'm afraid I can't help you, *amigo,*" said Blackwell. "I don't even know the man."

The grin was now a fixed, wooden grimace. "You do not believe that I, *Teniente* Maximo Novarro, am your friend?"

"I said we're pals."

"And I heard you, *amigo,*" said Novarro, "and I also heard the tone in which you expressed yourself. But, listen. I shall prove to you how magnanimous I am. I shall acquaint you with the profound depth of my friendship for you. Did you not kill a man, *un Méjicano,* here in the Granadas a few days ago?"

Novarro observed the look on Blackwell's face. "Ah?" said Novarro. "You do not deny? *¡Bueno!* In not denying, you do not antagonize me, and thus my friendship for you continues unabated. That Mexican you killed was one of my men, *amigo,* but I am not angry with you. Instead, I am grateful."

Blackwell said nothing. He was getting a hint of what lay ahead, and he did not like it. He felt the best thing to do would be to keep his mouth shut as much as possible.

When Blackwell did not speak, Novarro continued: "You

do not believe me, *amigo?* Listen to me. That man you killed was also a lieutenant in the indomitable army of our great republic. But he was a most selfish man. He and I were delighted to proceed into Los Estados Unidos under cover and apprehend Josélito. But this misbegotten son of doubtful parentage thought to apprehend secretly Josélito alone and then clasp all the honor to himself. He would become a captain, perhaps even a major, on the strength of such a marvelous exploit, the dirty pig! But you, *amigo,* foiled him, and, in foiling him, you have made it possible for me alone to attain the full measure of the reward for the capture of Josélito." His chest swelled, his eyes began to glitter with anticipation. "Think of it. Captain Maximo Novarro! At my age a captain! That is why my heart overflows with affection and brotherly feelings for you, *amigo.* Will you not tell me where to find Josélito?"

"I can't tell you," said Blackwell, "because I don't know."

"Liar!" growled Novarro.

Novarro signaled his men and barked several swift words of command. They seized Margarita Luz and carried her over to a rock. After untying her ropes, they laid her on her stomach across the stone. One of the men removed her vest while the other held her down. Only her shirt now covered the skin of her back.

"What are you going to do to her?" asked Blackwell. He could hear the dull beating of his heart.

"This," said Novarro. He turned on his heel and strode swiftly over to the rock. The quirt rose high in the air and then descended with all the strength of Novarro upon the back of Margarita Luz. She tried to stifle a moan, but still it crept out through gritted teeth.

Novarro now came back to Blackwell. The Mexican's eyes glittered cruelly. "You have seen what I intend to do," said Novarro. "I would prefer using the whip on you, but I know how you *yanquis* value and respect women, and so my ends will be better served by whipping her. It will be entirely up to you, *yanqui* . . . how many lashes she will have to endure. The moment you tell me where I may find that dog, Josélito, that very moment will the whipping of the *señorita* end, but not one moment before. Are we understood, *yanqui?*"

Blackwell almost felt like crying with helplessness and frustration. "I tell you, Novarro, I don't know. I hardly know this Josélito. I only saw him twice. I've got no idea whatever where he's at."

"I have had enough of your lies," snarled Novarro. "I know that Josélito is your friend. You killed a loyal, devoted soldier of our great republic to save the life of that foul pig. I have ways of finding out things. I know all about you and Josélito, *yanqui*. Now, one last time. Where is Josélito?"

"What if neither one of us knows?"

"Then that is most unfortunate for the *señorita*." Novarro turned on his heel and started for the girl.

"Wait!" Blackwell gathered himself and tried to throw himself up against Novarro's legs, but the ropes about Blackwell's wrists and limbs aborted the attempt. "Damn you, Novarro, wait!" shouted Blackwell, trying to kick out with his bound feet at Novarro.

Novarro adroitly avoided Blackwell's clumsy efforts. Novarro's boot lashed out, the sharp point of it gouging into the pit of Blackwell's stomach. Nausea rushed through Blackwell. He doubled over on the ground and retched, and, when he could see again through pained, tear-filled eyes, he watched as Lt. Novarro went about his grim task.

Blackwell closed his eyes. But he could not shut his ears. The quirt whistled and whined as it rose and fell. The girl made little outcry at first. She kept most of the agony locked behind clenched teeth, but still some of the anguish kept slipping through, and the sound of it tore at Blackwell's heart.

Novarro worked steadily and methodically, a definite rhythm in the swinging of his arm up and down. The quirt cracked and snarled while a fine film of sweat came out on Novarro's face. Not a sound came out of him, but he was in ecstasy. His mouth was parted in a grimace of glee; his black eyes glittered fiercely.

Blackwell began to curse. He tugged at his bonds, he strained until he thought his muscles would tear and part, but the ropes held. He wanted to keep his eyes closed, yet he couldn't, for now Margarita Luz was beginning to give voice to her torment.

Blackwell began to roll and heave himself along the ground. He did not exactly know what he had in mind—only some idea of bringing himself close enough to Novarro to kick out with his bound legs in the desperate hope of diverting Novarro a moment from his work. Blackwell had attained half the distance when the shooting began.

One of the soldiers holding the girl threw up his hands and clawed at his throat. The other soldier dove for his rifle that he had placed on the ground, but a slug smashed the back of his head. He dropped limp and unmoving on his weapon.

Novarro had dropped his quirt. He whirled, the pearl-handled pistol flashing in his hand, but, before he could fire, a bullet smashed him in the chest and rocked him back a step. The force of the blow caused him to relax his grip on his gun, and it fell to the ground.

Another shot blazed out. Novarro screamed, and his right arm hung limply at his side; the slug had shattered his shoulder. Novarro turned to run, blindly, reeling, panic-stricken. Another bullet smashed the other shoulder. He staggered and almost went sprawling, but at the last instant he recovered his balance and continued on his panicked, erratic, heedless flight.

Still another slug took Novarro in the back, bludgeoned him down on his knees not five feet from Blackwell. Novarro's eyes were distended with agony and the horrible imminence of death. *"¡Madre de Dios!"* he shrieked in supplication in what he must have known was the last instant of his life. The next slug crashed into the base of his skull. He pitched forward, his bleeding head just next to Blackwell. Blackwell rolled over once to get away from the blood of the *Teniente* Maximo Novarro.

Blackwell lifted his eyes and saw Josélito. The big Mexican was coming at a run, heading straight for the girl who was now struggling to sit up on the rock. Gunsmoke still swirled out of the muzzles of the two ornate .45s in his hands. He holstered the weapons as he reached the girl. She had just started to sit up, but she wavered and would have fallen had not Josélito been there to catch her. He handled her very tenderly, all the while crooning to her in a strangely gentle voice.

"My little one, my poor little one. Why did you not tell them? Why did you have to take all this punishment? I am not worth it, *pequeña*."

Margarita Luz started to smile up at Josélito, but a sudden spasm of pain turned the smile into a grimace. Josélito helped her to her feet, and this enabled Blackwell to see her back. The shirt was soaked with blood.

The girl wanted to walk, but Josélito would not let her. He lifted her in his arms and carried her over to the hut and set her down close to the wall. Josélito had a serape over one shoulder, and he wrapped this blanket about the girl's shoulders.

Only when the girl had assured him that she was all right did Josélito pay any attention to Blackwell. The big Mexican strolled over, the main focus of his attention on the dead body of Lt. Novarro. He towered above the dead man, quivering with rage.

"You will flog no more women, *tú chingando cabrón!*"

Finally Josélito shifted his attention to Blackwell. He drew his knife and slashed at the ropes binding Blackwell's legs.

"You did not tell them either, *amigo,*" said Josélito. He sounded pleased.

"I didn't tell them because I didn't know," said Blackwell through his teeth. "Damn you, Josélito! Why do you have to get a poor girl like that mixed up in your dirty politics? Aren't you man enough to leave her out of it? I'd have told Novarro if I'd known where you were hiding out."

A look of compassion and understanding came over Josélito's features as he cut the ropes around Blackwell's wrists.

"I was fortunate to arrive as soon as I did," said Josélito. "I was watching for something like this ever since you killed that other agent, *amigo*. I went to the house of Diego Luz, and he told me you had gone out to see Margarita. When I did not find you with the sheep, I followed the trail of five horses that led me here. I came as fast as I could, *amigo*."

Chapter Eleven

It was after he left Margarita and Josélito, that Blackwell spotted the rider. The ridge he had ascended flattened out to form a small, high mesa. The ground was barren of graze. Mesquite and the inevitable sage grew, but there was no other vegetation, only sage and mesquite and sand and rock, and the almost flat surface of the mesa. Off in the distance, at what apparently was the other end of the tiny plateau, the rider was motionless against the skyline. The fellow made no move to come ahead or go away.

Blackwell sat there in his saddle, undecided. Was this at last Chandler?

For perhaps five minutes, the rider and Blackwell regarded each other, both of them motionless and wary. Then, to see what would happen, Blackwell clucked his bay ahead.

The rider reacted instantly and swiftly. He stooped over in his saddle and then came up with a rifle. Blackwell saw the bright gleam of the sun on the blued barrel, and, as the weapon was thrown to the other man's shoulder, Blackwell ducked low over his saddle horn and reined the bay sharply to the side.

The rifle blasted. The bullet kicked up dirt five feet ahead of the bay. Then the rider lifted his sights and sent the next slug screaming over Blackwell's head.

Blackwell's own Winchester was out now. With his knees he stilled the jittery bay long enough to whip the rifle to his shoulder and slam out a shot. The attempt was hurried but still it was close to the mark. The rider on the blue roan plunged out of his kack.

The bay began to skitter around, and Blackwell had to let

go of his rifle with his left hand and grab the lines again, but, even so, the bay continued to snort and prance, and it was the constant movement that undoubtedly saved Blackwell's life. The slug that shrieked by him missed his head by no more than two inches.

Blackwell waited no more. He threw himself headlong out of the saddle as another bullet whined above him, and then he was hitting the ground, plowing up grit and sand that got between his teeth and into his eyes. He lay flat on his stomach while the bay, frightened, ran off a little, but then stopped when its forehoofs tramped on the trailing reins.

Blackwell dragged himself on his stomach behind the screening shelter of a mesquite. Then he began to wait. The sun had passed its zenith and was now a quarter of the way down to the horizon, but it still retained the full force of its heat.

Blackwell cursed and tried not to get impatient, but, as the time wore on with an interminable slowness, the urge to get it over with grew in him until it was almost uncontrollable. He brushed the Stetson from his head and this time ventured up high enough to take a look over the top of the mesquite bush.

He felt the slug flick at his hair and then the echoes of the gun blast began wailing over the mesa and spreading thinner and fainter across the empty land. Swiftly the second shot came, but Blackwell was already going down and this slug did not even come close.

The gunman at the other end of the mesa sprayed the mesquite with lead. The slugs whined and snarled and wood crackled as some of the twigs were snapped in two.

As he rolled, Blackwell screamed. He tried to put as much pain and mortal agony into the shrieks as he could. Then he choked them off abruptly, and kept on rolling. This time he stopped behind a flat slab of rock that was high enough to shield him while at the same time it afforded an impenetrable barrier against bullets. Then Blackwell started to wait again.

At last, he peeped cautiously above the surface of the rock. Outlined against the sky of the other end of the mesa, stood the gunman, rifle half raised to his shoulder as he carefully scanned the spot where Blackwell had been hiding. Suddenly the gunman broke and ran, and then Blackwell heard it, too—the snort of a laboring horse climbing the sharply sloping side of the mesa.

Blackwell jumped up and snapped the Winchester to his shoulder. The gunman was racing as fast as he could run. He had almost reached his blue roan. Blackwell fired. The shot missed. With a flying leap, the gunman vaulted over and above the rump of his horse and hit his kack. Flattening himself along the blue roan's neck, he spurred the horse into motion. Blackwell tried two more swift shots.

These also missed. There was not much to shoot at any more, and Blackwell held his fire. The blue roan galloped over the rim of the mesa and dropped from sight. Cursing, Blackwell began sprinting for his bay. As he ran, he threw one look at the rider who had come up behind him to frighten off the bushwhacker. The horseman was Josélito.

Blackwell wasted no time in explanations. His stride never broke as he raced toward the blaze-faced bay. He caught the lines and swung up in the saddle and began spurring the bay. The animal snorted, hesitated, and then broke into a swift, clattering run across the mesa. Blackwell became aware that Josélito was following him across the plateau on the big hammerhead roan.

When Blackwell reached the far end of the small mesa, he had to rein in the bay for a moment while he looked for the way down the sloping sides of the plateau. He spotted the trail almost instantly, and then Blackwell paused to search the land below for sign of the fleeing bushwhacker.

But the ground had turned hard and flinty, and the trail petered out. Blackwell reined in the sweating bay and dismounted to examine better the ground and then began beating the flat of his right hand against his chaps in disgust when he could perceive no further signs.

Josélito came up and reined in the roan. The big Mexican dropped swiftly to the ground and knelt on the earth and almost pressed his nose to the surface as he searched for markings on the rock. He had no more success than Blackwell. Then Josélito put his ear to the ground and listened with his mouth open. Finally he rose to his feet and looked at Blackwell. "We will catch him, *amigo,*" he said.

Chapter Twelve

The rest of that day Blackwell and Josélito tried to pick up the trail of the mysterious gunman without success. They continued looking until night fell, still without luck. The man on the blue roan, to all intents, had vanished into thin air.

That night the two men camped in a cañon deep in this isolated part of the Granadas. Blackwell did not like the idea of building a fire, but Josélito minimized the perils this might possibly create.

"Could it have been Chandler?" asked Josélito.

"Maybe," said Blackwell. "For a minute there I thought it was. Something about him was familiar. But I couldn't get a good look. It could have been Chandler or someone else I know."

"Who else?" asked Josélito.

"I don't know," said Blackwell, and clammed up. That was the question he had been asking himself the past several hours. If the bushwhacker hadn't been Chandler, then who was he? Bobby Sheppard? Frank Richmond? Or, maybe, Angel Dawson? It was this last thought that turned Blackwell's guts cold. It even made him a little glad he hadn't killed the mysterious assailant.

"What do we do tomorrow, *amigo?*"

"Look for Chandler," said Blackwell wearily.

"Do you have any idea where to look?"

"I think he's at Lazy S," said Blackwell. "Lazy S is mixed up in the death of Gómez, and so that would be the best place for Chandler to hide out. He knows I wouldn't dare go there looking for him, not after killing Tex Hogarth. You wouldn't dare go there, either, Josélito. You'd be cut down before you even saw the headquarters of Lazy S."

"What are we to do, then?"

When Blackwell spoke, he murmured more to himself than to Josélito. "Crabtree."

"What did you say, *amigo?*"

Blackwell stirred a little. He said in a louder voice: "Fred Crabtree. He's a drunk who knows something about Chandler. In fact, Chandler stays with him every once in a while. I got Crabtree to spill a little something to me, but I didn't get very far." He did not mention Angel Dawson.

"Cheer up, *amigo,*" said Josélito, smiling brightly. "It is not as bad as you think. You have Josélito with you now. Together we will achieve wondrous results." He pulled the long knife from his sash and tested the edge with the ball of his thumb. "When I kiss this Crabtree with my *cuchillo,* he will talk. He will become most vociferous. My *cuchillo* never fails. Just you wait and see, *amigo.*"

The next afternoon, as they were approaching Crabtree's place, Josélito reined in his roan and held out a hand, halting Blackwell. The Mexican struck an attitude of intent listening.

After a while, Josélito said: "I do not like it."

They rode on far enough so that they could see that side of the house shaded by the cottonwoods. Two horses stood under one of the trees next to the well. One of the horses was the old grulla that belonged to Crabtree. The other was a blue roan.

At first sight of the blue roan, Blackwell froze in his kack. This was a stroke of luck he had not bargained for. He had become so accustomed to failure and disappointment that he had stopped believing there was anything else in store for him.

"That blue roan," said Blackwell. "The man who tried to

kill me yesterday rode a blue roan. I'm not saying he has the only blue roan in the Granadas. Maybe it's just a coincidence, but that could be the horse up there." He could no longer restrain his eagerness. "Let's go, Josélito."

Again Josélito struck out that detaining hand. "That would be most rash, *amigo,*" he said. "There should be two men in that house. Why do they not show themselves? Surely, they can see us."

"What do you think we should do?" asked Blackwell.

"We shall come in on the house from two directions. Observe those rocks over there at the bottom of the hill. They should be within rifle range. You will ride over there, and, when I begin to come in on the house, you shall dismount and race to the shelter of those rocks. If there is any shooting, you shall be in a position to distract and occupy one of the two in the house." The grin widened. "You have, perhaps, the more dangerous assignment, *amigo.*"

"That's what you say," snorted Blackwell, but he complied.

Josélito chuckled as Blackwell whirled the bay and sent it at a run in a wide circle, always out of rifle range of the house, until he had reached the hill. He stepped to the ground, his Winchester in hand, and glanced at the rocks, perhaps twenty feet ahead of him, and then at the house. Nothing stirred in or about the dwelling. There was one lone window in the front, none on this side or on the side from which Josélito would approach. The Mexican's plan was a sound one, Blackwell agreed to himself.

Now Blackwell glanced past the house to where Josélito sat his roan in the distance. The Mexican lifted an arm in signal, and then the man broke into a gallop and disappeared from sight. Blackwell could hear the thundering of hoofs as Josélito drove in on the house. He cocked the Winchester and, holding it at his hip, began to race toward the rocks.

He was halfway there when the shooting broke out. Apparently there were loopholes or cracks big enough to shoot out of in the siding of the house, and it was through an aperture like this that someone was throwing lead at Blackwell. The slugs whined and whistled about Blackwell's head; he could hear the angry, frustrated scream of each bullet as it missed its mark.

Blackwell threw himself on the ground and crawled the last five feet on his belly. The slugs began now to chew at the rocks behind which he lay. He could hear the sharp, steely whining as they ricocheted off the stones.

It seemed to Blackwell that another carbine was going inside the house beside the one spewing lead at him, and then still another gun joined in, fainter, as if from a greater distance. This, apparently, was Josélito joining the battle.

Blackwell hunched himself until he could peer a little around the edge of a rock. Then he poked out his rifle and levered three quick shots at the house. Wood splintered and cracked as the slugs smashed through the one-inch siding.

Suddenly someone began to shout in the house. The voice reached Blackwell faint with distance but still he could make out the words: "Stop! I quit! I quit! I've had enough!" The next instant a man came out the front door of the house, his hands held high above his head. Blackwell leaped to his feet and began running.

The fellow was Luke Chandler.

Chapter Thirteen

Blackwell could hear the pumping of his heart; his blood roared in his ears. Although he was running with all his speed, he thought he would never get there. He began to curse the high heels of his boots that made running so difficult.

Josélito came around the corner of the house. The two ornate .45s were in his hands, both weapons covering Chandler. As Blackwell came up, Josélito said: "This is one of the pigs. Look inside for the other one, *amigo*."

Blackwell tried to catch Chandler's eyes, but the man stood with hanging head. He pretended not to see Blackwell. Blackwell's mouth tightened, and he went over to the door and glanced inside.

Crabtree lay on his back in the middle of the floor of his filthy house. A great blotch of blood covered his puny chest and his knees were drawn up and his fingers were clawed at his breast as if he had died in extreme agony.

Blackwell turned from the door and walked slowly over in front of Chandler.

Josélito asked: "Who is this obscenity, *amigo?*"

Blackwell did not answer the query. He kept looking steadily at Chandler, but the man only stared at the ground. He still held his hands high, even though he was unarmed, and Blackwell could see a faint trembling in Chandler's knees.

Chandler was in his late thirties. He was a chunky man of medium height. He was bareheaded. His brown hair was thinning at the front. His face was red—the kind of complexion that never tans but turns pink or ruddy—and he looked sullen and whipped and scared.

At last, Blackwell said: "Long time no see, Luke."

Chandler said nothing.

Josélito said: "Luke? Luke Chandler?"

"That's right," said Blackwell.

"¡Chingando cabrón!" snarled Josélito, sheathing his six-shooter. Then the knife glittered suddenly in his hand. "Miguel Gómez was like a brother to me!" he shouted. "You hear, pig of a *gringo?*"

Josélito's eyes bulged and blazed;, his snarling, grimacing mouth made his face look uglier than ever. He raised the knife. The sun flashed brightly off the keen edge of the weapon.

"Josélito!" cried Blackwell, swinging his gun toward the huge Mexican and bringing him to a full stop.

At Josélito's first shout, Chandler's head darted up. A look of utter terror spasmed across his features. His mouth opened, and a shriek of fright erupted out of him. He crossed his arms in front of his face as if they could turn aside the keen point and edge of Josélito's knife.

Blackwell, holding back the glowering Josélito, said to Chandler: "Well, Luke, how long have you had that blue roan?"

Now that it appeared Josélito was not going to do anything to him, Chandler became sullen. He hooked his thumbs in his belt and kicked at the ground. He did not look Blackwell in the eyes.

"I just got him this morning," said Chandler.

"You're a god-damn' liar, Luke," said Blackwell.

"If you know more about it than I do, Tom, why do you want to ask me questions?"

Blackwell drew a deep breath. "All right," he said, "we'll take it your way. Who did you get the horse from?"

"What are you going to do to me, Tom?"

"That all depends on what you tell me."

"There's nothing to tell," said Chandler. "You know everything there is to know."

"How do you know what I know?"

"I saw the letter Richmond wrote to Nan. Then you came here and talked to Richmond. What else is there to know?"

"What happened to the money Jesse had on him?"

"I don't know. Gómez took it. He probably buried it before he was killed. Where it is now, nobody knows."

"Are you sure it was Gómez who robbed and killed Jesse?" asked Blackwell.

"I was then," said Chandler.

"How come Gómez didn't kill you, too? How come he left you alive to identify him? I don't think Gómez was that dumb."

Chandler looked defiantly at Blackwell. "Did you think I was standing there like a clay pigeon while Gómez was killing Jesse? I'll admit I turned yellow and ran. Jesse was not going to lose all that money without a fight. He jumped Gómez. While they were fighting, I turned and ran. It was dark, and, as soon as I got out of the light of the fire, Gómez couldn't find me any more. I heard a shot, and then someone hollered out like he was dying. That was Jesse. Gómez looked for me a while, but he couldn't find me. Then he rode off, and I went toward the fire and found Jesse dead." He inhaled deeply. "That's how it was, Tom."

"Wasn't Gómez masked?"

"What are you trying to do, Tom?" asked Chandler. "Take the side of a thief and a murderer?"

Josélito began to swear with great vehemence. Blackwell threw a look at the Mexican, but Josélito only stood there, cursing Chandler.

"I'm just thinking," said Blackwell, "that it's damn' funny

Gómez would rob someone with his face uncovered so he could be recognized. He wasn't an outlaw. He'd want to keep his identity a secret, wouldn't he? Why didn't he wear a mask, then?"

"Can't you see, Tom?" Chandler said, raising his voice. "Gómez killed Jesse. If he could have found me, he would have killed me, too. That's why he didn't wear a mask. He didn't have to because he didn't intend leaving any live witnesses behind."

"All right, Luke, I'll go along with you. Gómez killed Jesse. Now tell me this . . . where do Tex Hogarth and Bobby Sheppard come in?"

"Well," said Chandler, running his tongue over his lips, his eyes evasive again, "I ran into Tex Hogarth and Bobby Sheppard first thing the next morning while I was on the way to War Feather to report what happened. I told Hogarth and Sheppard, and they recognized Gómez from the description I gave them. They said that Gómez might try to skip the country into Mexico before the law got after him, so all three of us rode to where Gómez lived. When he saw me with Hogarth and Sheppard, Gómez figured he was done for. He tried to shoot it out. Hogarth and Sheppard plugged him before he could do any damage." Chandler threw a fearful look at Josélito. "I didn't fire a shot. Hogarth and Sheppard did all the shooting."

Josélito was breathing heavily. His big, wide-spaced teeth were bared in a snarl, but he kept himself in check.

"All right," Blackwell said again. "I'll still go along with you, Luke. But tell me this. When I came into the Granadas, why didn't you look me up and tell me all this? Why did you keep running from me?"

"I didn't have the guts to, Tom. I . . . I kept seeing Nan and little Davey, and then I remembered how you'd always been friends with Jesse, and I . . . I just couldn't bring myself to talk about it with you. I figured you could find out from Richmond everything you had to know and then you'd pick up and go back home."

Blackwell's tone grew thin and soft. "Why did you try to kill me?"

Chandler stood with his mouth open, saying nothing. He swallowed audibly. Panic flared in his eyes.

Blackwell's fingers tightened about the grip of the .44 that he still held in his hand. "I asked you a question, Luke," he said.

"I . . . I lost my head. I didn't mean to, but what else could I do? I saw you and this other *hombre* stop and look over the house a hell of a long time. Then you split and started coming in from two sides. You certainly can't call that peaceable and sociable. Me and poor Fred didn't know what to make of it. We . . . we only fired back in self-defense."

"You were waiting for me," said Blackwell, his voice hard. "You expected me and Josélito to ride right up to the door and then you were going to drop us in our tracks without a chance. Why?"

"No, no," whined Chandler. "You've got it all wrong. I've known you for years. We both worked for Jesse. Why would I want to do a thing like that?"

"Stop lying, Luke," said Blackwell, feeling the wrath pulsing at his temples. "You tried to gun me down yesterday, too. I know it was you because of the blue roan."

"Yesterday? Blue roan?" Chandler said blankly.

"On that tiny mesa," Blackwell elaborated. "You were masked, but I saw the blue roan."

"I think I know what you mean," said Chandler, "but you're all wrong. Maybe somebody on a blue roan tried to gun you, but that wasn't me. I don't own the only blue roan in the Granadas."

"I've had enough of your lies," said Blackwell.

"Lies? I swear it's all gospel truth. If you don't believe me, ask Richmond, ask Bobby Sheppard. If you hadn't killed Tex Hogarth, you could ask him, too. I've got someone to back me in everything I say!"

At this point, Josélito stepped forward. The knife was in his hand again, and he was testing the edge with the ball of his thumb. Chandler dropped back a step. Josélito looked at Blackwell and said quietly: "Let me kiss him with my *cuchillo, amigo*. I assure you he will speak the truth then."

Blackwell did not like the idea. He had no stomach for this sort of thing, but he had to find out something somehow. The conviction existed strongly in him that Chandler had lied. The man would not alter his story without persuasion. It was evident that Chandler was terrified of Josélito's ferocity, and this fear might break Chandler down. So Blackwell decided to go along with Josélito, just a little. He would stop Josélito, forcibly if necessary, if the Mexican started to go too far.

"Proceed, *amigo*," he said.

"Tom!" Chandler's face was gray with terror, his eyes bulged; they seemed on the verge of bursting out of their sockets. Great drops of sweat popped out on his face and trickled down his cheeks. "I've told you the truth!" he squawked hoarsely. "I've told you exactly what happened. I can't help it if Gómez did a thing like that. I can't be held responsible for what Gómez did or for what happened to him."

"Bueno," said Josélito with no compassion. "I shall now prick the skin."

He pressed on the knife, and a screech ripped out of Chandler. "Oh, God, I've told you the truth! How can I tell you anything else when what I've said is the truth?"

A vicious pleasure lighted Josélito's features. *"Bueno,"* he said again. "I shall now drive my *cuchillo* in a little deeper."

Just as Blackwell was about to intervene, Chandler began to screech. "No, no!" he screamed, pawing at Josélito. "I'll tell you. I'll tell you the truth. I'll tell you everything."

"Before I remove my *cuchillo,*" Josélito said mercilessly, "I wish to know this . . . did Miguel Gómez rob and kill the *Señor* Gray?"

"Oh, no, no. I had to say that. I was made to say that. Gómez didn't do it!"

"Who did it, Luke?" asked Blackwell.

"Hogarth. Tex Hogarth!"

At this moment Josélito released his grip on Chandler's shirt, and the man fell in a heap on the ground. He buried his face in his hands and began to sob rackingly

There was no pity, only revulsion, in Blackwell as he looked down on the man on the ground. "You know what you've done, don't you?" Blackwell said, his voice full of loathing. "You sent an innocent man to his death. Is that why you took to drink, Luke? The death of poor Gómez?"

"I can't be blamed for that," sobbed Chandler. He kept his face dug into his hands. "Gómez would have been killed one way or another. He was in the way of Lazy S. They wanted to get rid of him. So Hogarth and Sheppard killed Gómez and then threatened to kill me, too, if I didn't tell how Gómez robbed and killed Jesse first and then was shot down while he was trying to get away from Hogarth and Sheppard."

"It was Tex Hogarth who robbed and killed Jesse?"

"Yes."

"How did it happen?"

"Me and Jesse were camped in the Granadas when Hogarth and Bobby Sheppard rode up to our fire and asked if they could share our camp for the night. They appeared friendly, and me and Jesse happened to spill how he'd sold a big herd of cows and had eight thousand dollars on him.

Hogarth pulled a gun, and, when Jesse wouldn't give in, Hogarth killed Jesse. Sheppard had me covered, and I couldn't do anything."

Chandler paused, took a deep breath and continued. "Then Hogarth put it to me. He said he wouldn't kill me if I'd go along with him. He said there was a greaser named Gómez who owned some land that was too good to be wasted as sheep graze. Hogarth said he had been figuring for a long time on how to get rid of Gómez without getting into trouble. He told me that he and Sheppard were going to kill Gómez, and then I was going to ride to War Feather and report to the sheriff how Gómez had robbed and killed Jesse and then had been killed himself when Hogarth and Sheppard tried to arrest him." He swallowed hard. "They said that, if I didn't do it, they would kill me like they killed Jesse." He raised defiant eyes to Blackwell. "They meant it, too!"

"Why didn't you tell me that right off, Luke?"

"I told you why. I had to stay away from you. When it got around that you had come into the Granadas, Hogarth made it plain that, if I went to see you, he would kill me. I didn't dare let you find me, Tom! I want to live as much as anybody."

"I know," said Blackwell dryly. "You want to live so much you're willing to let innocent people die just to save your worthless hide. There's one more thing I want to know, Luke. Hogarth is dead. Why didn't you come to me with the truth after I'd killed Hogarth?"

"There's still Sheppard."

"You mean to say Bobby Sheppard has taken over where Hogarth left off? The kid hasn't got the guts or the brains to do a thing like that."

"Don't sell Bobby Sheppard short," said Chandler. "I know you've probably got him tallied as a dumb spoiled kid like everyone else, but he's mean, poison mean! He learned it by hanging around with Hogarth. It was Sheppard who told me to kill you because you were getting too nosey. He said, if I wouldn't do that, it would mean my life. It probably will, too," he said glumly. "Hogarth's dead, but Sheppard can always hire someone else to do his gun-throwing for him."

"If that's so," Blackwell said, "why did he give you the job of killing me? He should have known you were too dumb for it."

Chandler flushed. "Sheppard figured I could get you easier than anybody else. He said you wouldn't be expecting it from me. Not that I intended doing it that way," he hastened to add. "But when I saw you and Josélito sneaking up on the house, I didn't know what to make of it, and I lost my head and began shooting. But I only did it in self-defense, Tom!"

"Yeah," said Blackwell derisively. "Just one more question. Who's got Jesse's money?"

"I suppose Sheppard's got it now," said Chandler. "I don't know for sure. They never told me what they did with the money. All they said to me was play along with them or they would kill me." He lifted wide, appealing eyes to Blackwell. "What are you going to do with me, Tom? I told you everything. I kept my part of the deal. What are you going to do?"

"We're turning you over to Richmond," said Blackwell, "and you better not go back on what you told us, or we'll get you again, and the next time I won't stop Josélito from using his *cuchillo*. In fact, I'll get one for myself and give him a hand."

Chapter Fourteen

The next morning Blackwell, bitter and angry, rode out of War Feather and headed across the short stretch of desert toward the heights of the Granadas. Much had transpired while Blackwell had slept that night, after returning to his hotel room following the encounter with Chandler. It was the things that had happened that made Blackwell malevolent.

When Blackwell awakened that morning, he learned that Sheriff Richmond had gone out to Lazy S to serve his warrant on Bobby Sheppard, but Richmond had returned alone, saying that young Sheppard, forewarned of his impending arrest, had fled into the mountains. To Blackwell this all seemed very convenient and put up.

Then, too, that night while Richmond was gone from War Feather, someone had slipped a gun in to Luke Chandler in the county jail. Chandler had thrown down on the jailer, forced him to unlock the cell, and then Chandler, too, had fled, ostensibly into the Granadas.

So Blackwell rode, bitter and raging, for the mountains to try to do it all over again so far as Chandler was concerned. Only this time, Blackwell promised himself he was not going to observe the niceties of the law and human decency. He was going to adopt the brutal but effective and conclusive methods of Josélito.

He passed the rim of the desert about ten o'clock that morning, and by noon he was already high up in the mountains. He was pushing the bay mercilessly, treating the animal more harshly than he had ever treated any horse. There was no pity or forbearance in Blackwell this morning.

Finally, when the bay stumbled once and almost went

down on its fore knees, Blackwell reined in the weary horse. The animal was blowing hoarsely; its sides were dark and wet with sweat. Blackwell dismounted and patted the horse's neck, and then he took his canteen and wetted his bandanna and used the moist cloth to wash out the bay's mouth and nostrils. Then he poured a little water from the canteen into the horse's mouth.

He had prudently halted the bay on a high stretch of ground that was open all around. It was thus that Blackwell spied the horseman below, working up the rather steep pitch of the slope to come to him. Blackwell eyed first the horse and saw that it was a beautiful Arabian. Then Blackwell studied the rider. It was Angel Dawson.

Blackwell's first impulse was to mount his bay and ride off without waiting for the girl, but then he reasoned that, if she intended talking to him, she would stick doggedly to his trail until she managed to catch up with him. So Blackwell decided it was best to wait and have it over with.

The Arabian gained the same level of ground as Blackwell, and the girl reined in the horse about twenty feet away. She stepped down lithely from the saddle and dropped the lines to the ground. The Arabian stood with hanging head, flanks heaving.

Angel Dawson hooked her thumbs in her shell belt and came striding over to Blackwell, the sun glinting brightly off the yellow of her hair.

"You're still here in the Granadas."

"It looks like it, doesn't it?" said Blackwell quietly.

"You promised me you were leaving. You promised me that several days ago."

"And you promised to go with me."

"You could have written to me. You could have sent for me once you were in Colorado."

"Would you have come?"

"If you'd kept your part of the bargain . . . yes." After a pause, she said: "It's not too late . . . yet. We could go together . . . if you still want me."

The longing rose in Blackwell. He could feel it fill his throat. But at the same time the poison grew stronger and more invidious in his mind. Sadly he realized he could not get rid of the suspicion in him.

"Why would you go away with me?" he asked.

"Because I love you."

"Is that the only reason?"

"Isn't that reason enough?"

"If I went away," he said stiffly, "that would make it pretty convenient for the *hombre* or *hombres* behind the death of Gray, wouldn't it?"

"I'm only thinking of you," the girl said. She came ahead now and laid a hand on his arm. Her fingers pressed tightly against his flesh. "You're been lucky so far. You've come out of everything without a scratch. You won't be lucky forever."

"Is that a threat?" he asked.

"Threat?" she repeated. "I don't get what you mean, Blackwell."

"You get it all right," he said. "How dumb do you think I am, Angel? Every time I see you, it's always the same thing. You want me to give up what I'm doing. You want me to go back to Colorado. You say you want me to do these things because you're afraid I'll get killed if I keep on poking around. You say you love me. All right, I'll buy that. But there's another way of tallying this herd. If I quit and go home, what about the *hombre* who really killed and robbed Gray? What about Chandler and young Sheppard? They'd have nothing more to worry about if I went back to Colorado, would they? That would make it just fine and dandy for everyone who had a hand in the killing of Jesse Gray."

He reached out suddenly and closed a hand about her arm and squeezed with all the rage and hurt in him. "Who's behind it, Angel? Who's behind Chandler and Sheppard?"

"You're hurting me," she moaned.

"Tell me, Angel," he said through his teeth, "tell me."

"Oh, Blackwell, Blackwell," she cried. "Why can't you trust me? Why must you be so bitter and full of hate? I don't know anything about Chandler or Bobby Sheppard or their connection with Gray's death. Why won't you believe me? I love you, Blackwell, I love you!"

"That's not enough. You know more about this thing than you admit. Who put up Chandler and Sheppard?"

"I love you," she whispered doggedly.

"Quit that," he said angrily. "I know you love me. Now tell me who wants me out of the Granadas?"

A swift change came over Angel Dawson. The tears abruptly ceased. All the wincing passed from her features, and, if she was experiencing any hurt from his grip on her, she was now enduring it stolidly and unflinchingly. Those gray eyes became cold and calculating.

"Why do you keep saying there is someone behind Chandler and Bobby Sheppard?" Her voice was low.

With the pretense gone from her, Blackwell loosed his fingers from her arm. She pulled it quickly away and began rubbing the spot where he had held her.

"Neither Chandler nor Sheppard has the brains to plan anything like this," said Blackwell. "There has to be someone behind them. Who is he, Angel?"

She tossed her head. "You've got a pretty lively imagination, Blackwell. This was all Tex Hogarth's idea. Hogarth ran Lazy S. Bobby Sheppard thought the sun rose and set on Hogarth. There was nothing Bobby wanted to be more than a tough gunman just like Hogarth. Hogarth capitalized on the kid's weakness. He led Bobby around by the nose. Sure, the Sheppards own Lazy S, but it was really Hogarth's spread. He planned the killing and robbing of Gray just for an excuse to get Mike Gómez out of the way and then take over Gómez's place. Hogarth had ambitions of taking over every ranch in the Granadas. Now he's dead, and it's ended. You've avenged Gray. Why don't you go home?"

"If Hogarth was behind everything, then there's no danger for me if I keep poking around. With Hogarth dead, why should there be?"

She did not answer immediately. He could almost hear the wheels going around in her head as she thought over what she would say next. Finally she drew a deep breath and said: "You're either dumber or more bull-headed than I thought, Blackwell. You've got the crazy idea that there is a mysterious someone behind Gray's death so you'll keep going around, accusing people. One of these days you're going to accuse the wrong man, and he'll put a bullet in you. That's the reason I want you to drop this foolish, dangerous thing and take me to Colorado with you."

She reached up and caught the lapels of his jacket and pressed herself close to him. Her mouth was not far from his; he could feel her breath on his lips. Her eyes were very sober and grave.

"I won't get sentimental with you any more, Blackwell. I won't tell you any more that I love you. I'm here. I'm willing to go away with you. What are you going to do about it?"

There was a challenge in her eyes. Her warmth as she pressed against him had inflamed Blackwell's brain. He felt all his good intentions slipping, he felt the ache grow in his throat, and the knowledge came to him that this would probably be the last time he could embrace her like this. There was no future for him with her, no matter how much he loved her. So he put all the distrust and suspicion aside for a while. He bent his head and closed his arms about her. He felt very sad and mournful inside.

Chapter Fifteen

The sensation grew in Blackwell that he was not very far from the end of this matter. The feeling depressed rather than cheered him. He could not shake the premonition that, when he arrived at the conclusion, it would be an unpleasant and distasteful thing to him.

He rode deeper into the Granadas, ever searching. He felt tired and discouraged, but there was that certainty in him that, if he looked a little longer, he would find what he was seeking. Chandler's escape from jail and Sheppard's flight into the Granadas—if this latter were true—seemed to indicate that in their panic the two were heading for whoever had motivated them and to obtain this unknown man's counsel.

The panic and apparent incompetence of both Chandler and Sheppard might prompt whoever it was behind them to come into the open to settle things himself. This was what Blackwell was hoping for. This was why he had kept riding the Granadas.

All that morning he did not see a single living thing, neither human nor animal except a vulture once wheeling like a portent of doom high in the brown sky. When the sun had arrived at its zenith, Blackwell spotted the rider.

The horseman came loping up the sandy floor of a narrow valley, raising a tiny spume of dust behind him. Even at a distance, Blackwell recognized horse and rider. It was Luke Chandler on the blue roan. Since Chandler was heading for him, Blackwell reined in the bay and waited. This was one time Chandler was not trying to avoid him.

He hitched around in the saddle and gave a good look all about him. The land lay empty and desolate in his gaze.

There was sage and greasewood and ocotillo but no living thing outside of Chandler and his horse. There was no place, apparently, from which a hidden gunman could shoot him down while he was engaged in talk with Chandler. Nevertheless, the uneasiness persisted in Blackwell.

He watched with narrowed eyes and suspicious mind while Chandler reined in the blue roan ten feet away. There was a strange graveness in Chandler's face today. The cringing weakness seemed to be gone from the line of his mouth. He looked like a man who had made a long and thorough search of his soul and had finally arrived at a grim, unpleasant conclusion.

"You got over your bashfulness all of a sudden, didn't you?" Blackwell asked wryly.

"This is no time to be funny," said Chandler in a strange, calm tone. "I'm going to kill you, Tom."

Blackwell pulled up stiff and taut in his kack. "Thanks for telling me," he said quietly. "I kind of expected it, but I thought it was going to be tried from behind again."

Chandler flushed a little. "I'm not scared," he said. "I can take you."

"Are you sure there's no one behind me . . . to kind of help you out? Is that why you're so brave all of a sudden?"

"Do you think I haven't got any guts at all, Tom? I'll show you. I know I've done some dirty things since I came into the Granadas with Jesse. But that's all over. I'm through sneaking around. I'm through having things on my mind. From now on I do everything in the open, face to face." He swallowed hard. "Even if it means my death, I'm still doing it face to face."

"Who sent you, Luke?"

"Someone smarter than you," said Chandler.

"Who? Give me a name!"

Blackwell's anger and vehemence seemed to please Chandler. "It's someone you'll never guess. He's too smart for you, Tom."

"Who is he?"

"God damn you," said Chandler, "you'll never get his name from me. And don't think it's because I might be afraid I can't beat you. I can and I will. What makes you think you're so good with an iron?"

"I beat Hogarth," said Blackwell quietly.

"That doesn't mean a thing."

"Let's cut this tomfoolery, Luke. You know I can outdraw and outshoot you any day. You know you haven't a chance against me. Let's get together and talk some sense. For Nan and Davey. They need that eight thousand dollars. They need it bad." His voice was gentle and persuasive. "What do you say, Luke?"

Chandler's eyes became evasive. A look of shame and regret came over his face. "It's too late," he muttered.

"No, it isn't," said Blackwell. "You can still set things right. Maybe not for Jesse. But you can do something for Nan and Davey. Tell me who's behind it, and tell me where to find that money. You can square yourself a little that way.

Chandler began shaking his head violently. "You don't understand," he said. "You've got no idea what it's like. I'm in too deep. I've got to go the rest of the way. Dammit, Tom, don't you think I'm sorry? But I let myself be talked into it, and now it's too late. I've got no one to blame but myself." He paused and drew a deep breath. "I've got my orders and those orders are to kill you or be killed myself. I was told to trick you, to pretend that I meant no harm and, when you weren't looking, to let you have it."

Chandler's face turned gray and sick. "But I can't do it

like that. Not after what I went through because of poor Gómez. It would be a lot worse if I did it like that to you. Maybe I haven't a chance against you, but I don't care. I don't care about anything any more." He settled himself in his saddle and shifted slightly so that the holster at his right hip hung low and free. The muscles along Chandler's jaw bulged tense and hard.

Blackwell knew that it was coming soon. He also knew that he could no longer forestall it. Yet he tried. He said: "Listen to me, Luke. You're making too much of it. It can't be as bad and hopeless as you think. Listen, I. . . ."

"It's no good talking," Chandler cut in sharply. "I'm not going to jaw any more with you. I just want to tell you this. If I get you, that will be that. But if you get me and you happen to make it home, tell Nan and Davey I was sorry. That's all, Tom," he said with a grim finality.

There was nothing to do now but wait out these last few, excruciating, interminable seconds. Wait while the ugly resolution flared in Chandler's eyes. Wait while the blood drained from his face and his lips thinned with determination and the chords in his neck and the fingers of his right hand curled and hooked.

Then Luke Chandler went for his gun.

There was a desperate, pressing hurry in Chandler's movements. He clutched hard at the gun handle and jerked the weapon up out of the holster. With all the speed he could muster, he brought the .45 up to a level, the gaping, hungry bore searching for Blackwell.

Blackwell's .44 lay cold and heavy in his hand, the seven-and-a-half-inch barrel aimed at Chandler's chest. As Chandler's weapon steadied, Blackwell fired. The Colt roared and bounced in his hand.

Chandler uttered a cry. His gun blasted, but the slug

slammed into the ground. The recoil knocked the .45 out of his hand.

Chandler's head folded down slowly over his chest as if he were extremely tired and was in the act of dozing off. For several seconds he sat in his saddle like that, head inclined, chin against his neck, then slowly and gently he began to bend forward. He went down like that until his stomach ground against the saddle horn, and then, with a choked cry, Chandler rolled sideways out of the kack. A small cloud of dust popped up where he hit the ground.

Blackwell stepped quickly down off the bay, the .44 still in his hand. He ran over and dropped to his knees beside Chandler, who lay on his back.

Chandler still lived, but, looking at the blood gushing out of the wound in the man's chest, Blackwell knew he did not have far to go. Already that waxen pallor was crawling over Chandler's face. His open eyes stared fixedly up past Blackwell, not seeing him at all, seeing only the swift, terrifying approach of death.

"Luke," said Blackwell hopelessly. The focus of Chandler's eyes moved and settled on Blackwell's face.

Chandler made no attempt to speak. He went on staring up at Blackwell with that blank, uncomprehending fixity.

Blackwell tried again. "For Nan and Davey, Luke. For them, tell me who's behind it. Tell me where the money is."

Chandler's lips fluttered. He tried to articulate something, but only strangled sounds emanated from his throat. He sensed the nearness of death and this gave him a final frantic burst of strength. He came halfway up on his elbows with the effort, eyes distending. He gasped two words and then fell back, dead.

To Blackwell, the words had sounded like Triste Cañon.

Chapter Sixteen

In the middle of the next morning, Blackwell came across the tracks of a horse apparently headed into the fastnesses of the Granadas. As this was the first sign he had encountered since burying Luke Chandler, Blackwell began following the tracks. They looked to be quite fresh.

The tracks went at a slant down the mountainside, clinging always to the more friendly pitches and slopes, and if whoever had laid these tracks had negotiated a way down, Blackwell felt he could do the same. The bay was sure-footed and did not have too much difficulty although several times it had to slide down a steep bank on its haunches. But the bay finally reached the level ground.

Blackwell turned in the saddle once and gave a look up the way he had just come. If someone had been watching, then he had been seen coming down the mountainside. The tracks he was following led straight into the junipers ahead.

The junipers apparently were deserted, but Blackwell no longer was willing to go by the evident appearance of things. The tracks swerved now to the left, and Blackwell turned the bay with them. He presumed that he was in the center of the grove when he abruptly came upon the tiny clearing.

The ground was gray. There was a jumble of stones, and in the middle of these a tiny spring sparkled. There was also a horse in the clearing, a handsome palomino wearing a silver-studded saddle and bridle. Sleeping on the ground by the spring was Bobby Sheppard.

The boy lay on his side with his head pillowed on his hands. He slept heavily, his mouth open, his breathing loud and regular. His face was slack with exhaustion, an image of the strain he had experienced the past few days. His fancy clothing was soiled. A light tawny fuzz covered the tip of the boy's chin and his upper lip. He was utterly unaware of Blackwell's presence.

As he stared down at the sleeping boy, a huge disgust and loathing came to Blackwell. This boy's life was a futile thing. All that he had contributed in nineteen or twenty years of living was an immeasurable amount of suffering and heartbreak for his father.

Never taking his glance off young Sheppard, Blackwell stepped down from the bay. The cinches squeaked mournfully and loudly in all the stillness, but the boy slumbered on. Holding the .44 in his right hand, Blackwell bent over and with his left scooped up a fistful of sand. He tossed this at Sheppard. The boy groaned and then awoke suddenly, sitting bolt upright, mouth gaping with surprise, eyes batting furiously.

When Sheppard saw Blackwell and the gun in his hand, the boy's face turned white. He swallowed with difficulty and then caught hold of himself and pulled his lips in tightly against his teeth.

Blackwell said: "What are you doing here, Sheppard?"

The boy had to clear his throat twice before he could articulate any words. "I'm just riding through," he said.

"Through to where?"

"I don't know. Just through, I guess."

"I want to know, kid."

"Honest, I'm just riding through. That's the truth."

"You're not sassy any more, are you?"

The boy hung his head. "I'm sorry, Blackwell. I apologize. I was drunk that day in the Longhorn. I didn't know what I was saying or doing. I'm sorry."

"You don't have any guts, either," said Blackwell with contempt. "It's just as well. You'll tell me all the quicker what

I want to know and save yourself a lot of grief. Where are you headed for, kid? Who are you going to see?"

"I'm not going anywhere in particular. I'm just running. I'm running from you."

"I know that," said Blackwell stiffly. "But you're going to see someone. Luke Chandler told me there is someone behind you. If there wasn't, you'd have stayed on Lazy S."

Fright whitened the boy's lips. "There's no one behind me, Blackwell. I'm not going to see anyone. Honest! I didn't stay at Lazy S because it wouldn't do any good any more. Richmond couldn't keep you away forever. There's a warrant out for me. Someway, somehow, you'd get to Lazy S. I knew it, so I ran. I went on the dodge. I came here because this is the most deserted part of the Granadas. I was sure I had lost you. I was so tuckered out I fell asleep, and that's how you caught me. That's the truth, Blackwell."

"What about this *hombre* that Chandler told me is behind you and him?"

The boy's eyes were luminous with fear. "Where is Chandler?" he asked.

"I killed him."

The boy bit down hard on his lower lip. A small, whimpering sound slipped between his lips.

"Are you going to tell me, kid?" asked Blackwell, glaring coldly down at young Sheppard.

"I don't dare," whined the boy.

"Why don't you dare?"

"He'd kill me if I did!"

"And I'll kill you if you don't."

A violent shudder ran through the boy. He lifted a strained, despairing face up to Blackwell. "Why should I talk?" he asked dully, his fear-stricken eyes already accepting the inevitable. "Either way, I'll be killed."

"Not if you tell me, you won't be killed," said Blackwell. His voice became low and reassuring. "Look, kid. I'm satisfied that Hogarth killed Gray. I'm satisfied that you just happened to be with Hogarth, and so far as avenging Gray is concerned, I'll pass over you. I mean it, kid. All you have to do is tell me who this *hombre* is that planned the killing of Gray. Tell me that and I'll be through with you. You can take your horse and gun and ride away from here."

"All right, I'll tell you." He paused and licked his lips nervously. "You probably won't believe me."

At this instant Sheppard's eyes looked past Blackwell, and what the boy saw threw a terrible, frenzied fear into him. His eyes distended, his mouth gaped in a tongueless cry, and he flung up his hands. Then the shot rang out.

The slug slammed young Sheppard backward. The life went suddenly out of his eyes, and he hit the ground with a thud and lay there unmoving as the echoes of the shot went rolling through the junipers and away up the mountainside.

Blackwell was caught helplessly with the cocked .44 in his hand. He had felt the breath of the bullet pass him the instant before the slug had smashed into the boy. Now Blackwell stood there, his insides crawling, waiting for the second slug to crash into him. But it did not come.

Slowly the realization came to Blackwell that he was not marked down for a bullet—yet. He did not have to be told what to do with his gun. He opened his fingers and watched the .44 drop to the ground. Then, his hands held shoulder high, Blackwell carefully turned.

What he saw gave him the greatest shock of his life. On the moment his vision blurred and the world seemed to rock all about him and he felt as if the bottom had dropped out of his stomach.

At the edge of the junipers, smoking gun pointed steadily and menacingly at Blackwell's belly, stood Jesse Gray.

Chapter Seventeen

After a moment, Gray started walking in, the rowels of his spurs dragging in the sand, the high, pointed heels of his boots sinking into the soft, gray grit. The gun in Gray's hand never once wavered out of line with the center of Blackwell's abdomen. There was a small, quizzical smile on Gray's mouth.

By now the shock had passed from Blackwell. He felt the first dark stirrings of rage inside him as the scope of the plot began to dawn on him. His breaths commenced coming in measured, wrathful gasps. His fists clenched. The line of his lips was pinched and bitter.

Blackwell in his surprise had lowered his arms, but Gray did not mind, for Blackwell's gun lay at his feet and Gray's iron was in his fist and cocked and aimed. Gray came to a stop just beyond Blackwell's reach.

"Hello, Tom, old kid," said Gray. His eyes glittered with a lucent malevolence. "You can relax. I'm no ghost."

"You dirty pig!" said Blackwell.

The smile faltered, then flared wider and brighter and more venomous on Gray's mouth. He was a tall man, as tall as Blackwell, with wide shoulders and the narrow waist and flat hips of a horseman. His face was very handsome. He had bright blue eyes and two long dimples in his cheeks and a finely chiseled nose. The hair that showed under his flat-crowned black hat was red and so was the mustache that dropped down around the corners of his mouth. The mustache was something new.

Gray was wearing a black flannel shirt and over this a blue and white checkered woolen jacket. Black woolen trousers were tucked into the tops of his boots. The gun in his hand was a .44 Remington conversion.

Slowly the smile died on Gray's lips, and a chilling, naked sobriety came over his features. "I'd put a bullet in you right now, Tom," he said, "but I want to talk with you first. I'm not going to stand here with a gun on you while I talk. You've come too damn' close to spoiling everything for me, so I'm not going to take any chances."

Still keeping the gun on Blackwell, Gray stepped over to the bay and took the lariat off the saddle. Then he made Blackwell turn around, and, when this was done, Gray dropped the loop over Blackwell and pulled it tight about his arms. Blackwell then was made to lie on the ground while Gray firmly and securely trussed his legs.

This done, Gray sighed and, holstering his gun, began building a smoke, all the while squatting in front of Blackwell and watching him with an intent, calculating stare. Gray rolled his cigarette, licked paper, and smoothed the tiny cylinder, then popped it into his mouth and struck a match. Only when he ducked his head a little to light the smoke did his eyes break from Blackwell's face.

Gray exhaled a great cloud of smoke and said: "How's Davey, Tom?" There was a small catch in his voice.

"You low-down, stinking skunk!" said Blackwell.

Gray flung away his cigarette, and then, in the same motion, brought the back of his hand across Blackwell's face. "Did you hear me? I want to know how Davey is! He's my son. God damn you! Tell me about Davey!"

Blackwell's face tingled and ached where he had been struck. He was quivering with helpless fury. He pursed his mouth and spat up into Gray's face.

"You're still alive, Tom," said Gray, voice thick with emotion, "only because I want to know about Davey."

"Why should I tell you?" said Blackwell. "After I tell you, you'll probably kill me. So why should I say anything to you?"

"If you don't tell me, I'll kill you anyway," said Gray, "only I'll make sure you won't die a quick, easy death. I'll plant a couple of slugs in your belly and maybe another one in your spine for good measure, and then I'll hang around for a few hours, watching you die."

The tone of it struck a chill in Blackwell. Gray sounded as if he meant it, and, remembering everything that had happened since Gray had come to the Granadas, Blackwell had no doubt that Gray would do what he had said.

"I'll make a deal with you, Jesse," he said. "I want to know a few things before I die. I want to know why you've done what you've done. After you've told me, I'll tell you about Davey."

Gray considered this. Finally he reached a decision. "All right, I'll tell you." He paused before proceeding. His glance lifted and looked beyond Blackwell as if considering carefully what he was about to say. "I don't suppose you'll understand, Tom," he began, "but it makes little difference whether you do or don't. I'm not a bad husband. I'm not a bad father. I loved Nan, and I tried to do right by her. I love Davey." That catch came into his voice again. "There's nothing I love in the world more than my son . . . except one woman, and it isn't Nan."

He edged a little closer to Blackwell and spread a hand as if by that gesture he could express himself more adequately. "You can't understand that, because you could never love anyone the way I do. I'm not a killer, yet I've killed and I'll kill again and I'll keep on killing as long as there is a breath of life in me. I'll do all that killing just to have that woman. Would you do that, Tom? Would you kill me just to have a woman, a woman you loved?" Gray shook his head. "No. You can't love that way. I'm not saying that you couldn't love a woman and love her fiercely, but there's a limit to what you would do for her. That's the way you're made. You're tough and proper, very proper."

Gray drew a deep breath. His eyes seemed to be pleading with Blackwell to understand. "I guess the simplest thing would have been to run off with her. I'd have done that, too, except for you. You love Nan. You'd never stand for anyone doing a thing like that to your sister. You'd have hunted me down until you found me and killed me."

"This woman you're talking about," said Blackwell, "is Angel Dawson, isn't it?"

"It is," said Gray. "I met her almost two years ago on that cattle buying trip I took to Wyoming. I tried to forget her, I tried to fight what I felt for her, but it was no dice, Tom," he said, shaking his head. "I didn't have the heart to tell Nan. Then there was Davey, and I thought that would hold me back, but, when it came down to choosing between Davey and Angel, I had to pick Angel."

His eyes were slitted and cold and unpenitent as he stared at Blackwell. "You were the big stumbling block. I had to fix it so you would be satisfied and would not spend the rest of your life hounding me. I know you, that's just what you would have done if I'd up and run away from Nan." He paused and breathed deeply. "I had to make you believe that I was dead. I couldn't just disappear, understand. I had to have proof that I was dead, a witness who saw me die. So I worked on Luke Chandler until I got him to come around to it. I kept in touch with Angel. Her letters to me came in an envelope addressed to Luke. She was supposed to be his sister, just so no one would suspect anything. When the time was ready, she came here to the Granadas to set everything up.

"It was a good idea, it was perfect," he boasted. "Angel

found the Sheppard kid and got to work on him. There was Hogarth who was an ambitious man. He dreamed of someday owning all the rangeland in the Granadas. Hogarth was the real power behind Lazy S. He was clever, but me and Angel used him, too. She laid our plan in front of Hogarth. Someone had to kill me for the money I had on me and then Hogarth could kill that *hombre* and claim he had done it to keep the thief and murderer from getting away. This *hombre* could be someone who was in Hogarth's way. So Hogarth picked Gómez. Me and Luke picked up a drifter and took him into the Granadas with us. I killed that drifter, and that's the corpse that was hauled into War Feather and buried as me. Luke Chandler identified it as me and who was there around to say otherwise? Hogarth and Sheppard then killed Gómez. The perfect set-up!"

"Except for the eight thousand dollars," said Blackwell.

"It's my money, isn't it?" he cried, as if trying to justify what he had done. "I need a stake to settle down with Angel. It's not like stealing, is it?"

"No, it isn't," said Blackwell, sick inside. "It's just plain murder, you son-of-a-bitch!"

Gray's hand started to lift again, but he checked himself. "I'll let it pass," he said stiffly. "You won't call anybody names much longer."

"You should have known you couldn't get away with it," said Blackwell.

"Who says I couldn't get away with it? I'm getting away with it right now, ain't I? I'll admit it hasn't come off as smooth as I had planned. It's that damn' Luke Chandler's fault. I knew you would come to find out what had happened when word got back home that I was dead. I planned for that. All Luke had to do when you came to the Granadas was to tell you that I was dead and the money was gone and the *hombre* who had killed me was taken care of. But Luke turned yellow on me. He got to brooding about how Gómez was shot down without a break. He brooded about Nan and Davey. He started hitting the bottle, and I couldn't risk him any more. So I had him lay low while you found out from others what had happened. But you wouldn't go for it, and that's just too bad for you." His eyes speared at Blackwell. "I'm waiting to hear about Davey," he said.

"You're not through telling me what I want to know," Blackwell said evenly. "How many times did you try to have me killed, Jesse?"

"I tried everything I knew to discourage you and to scare you off. I let you be until you went to see Crabtree. The old soak didn't know anything. He was just a drinking partner of Luke's, and I encouraged Luke to do his drinking there instead of in town where he might spill something and you don't know who might pick it up. Angel tried to talk you out of it, after Crabtree's, but she told me you'd never give up. Then Hogarth said he'd fix you, and I let him go ahead. But you beat Hogarth. So I tried Novarro."

"Novarro?"

"Sure," said Gray. "Do you think I've been hiding myself in a cave or something? Nobody knows me here. I've been moving about the Granadas free as you please. I'm not Jesse Gray in these mountains. I'm John Grant. But to get to Novarro. I kept a close watch on you, Tom, when you first came into these mountains. I was always behind you, trailing you. I saw you kill that Mexican who tried to kill Josélito. Then I found out about Novarro and why he had come here. So I tipped him off that you and this Margarita Luz knew where Josélito was hiding out. I figured on Novarro killing the two of you and taking both you troublemakers off my hands, but that fell through."

"So you took a crack at me yourself. That was you on the blue roan that day on the mesa, wasn't it?"

"How did you know?"

"I just put two and two together," said Blackwell. "In fact, I can mostly tell you the rest. After Josélito scared you off at the mesa, you turned the blue roan over to Luke Chandler so I would think he was the bushwhacker. You also ordered him to kill me, but instead me and Josélito put Luke in jail. Who helped him break out?"

"Angel slipped Luke the gun. I was always afraid that he would squeal, so I wanted him out of jail. I decided to give him one more chance. I told him to kill you, and, if he failed this time, I'd kill him. I explained to him how to do it over and over so that even a blockhead would understand. All he had to do was to ride up to you and pretend he was going to tell you everything. Then, when you were off guard, he was to pull his gun and plug you." He made a wry, disgusted face. "What went wrong?"

"Luke decided to be a man," Blackwell said. "He was through with sneaking and back-stabbing. He faced me, and we had it out fair and square. He died like a man. You didn't deserve the loyalty he gave you. After the way you pushed him around, he still wouldn't tell on you. You're a filthy dog, Jesse!"

Gray's lips pinched sullenly, wrathfully. "You ready now to tell me how Davey is?" he asked.

Blackwell was trying to spar for time, but there were not many more minutes that he could hope to gain. He had been tugging all the while at his bonds, but there was no give to them. Even if there was, Gray was too close and watchful.

He nodded at the dead boy who lay to one side. "What about Sheppard? Where did he fit in?"

A look of contempt came over Gray's features. "He was

just a fool kid who was used by Hogarth and Angel. He was a loud-mouth and a braggart and yellow besides. He went all to pieces after Luke was put in jail and implicated the kid in the killing of Gómez. I told him to sit tight, that he had nothing to worry about, but he got panicky and ran into the mountains." He threw a scathing look at the dead boy. "I knew all along I would have to kill him to make sure he wouldn't spill anything. I'm glad it's over." He paused. "How's Davey? How's my son?"

Blackwell knew he did not have long to go. There was no fear of death in him, but he hated to go like this, all trussed up and helpless and unable even to try to hit back. He felt cold and futile inside.

"What about Nan?" he asked. "Aren't you interested how she is?"

"Nan doesn't mean anything to me any more," said Gray. "I just want to know about Davey. Tell me how he looked the last time you saw him. Does he still remember me?" Gray's voice was wistful. "Does he ask for me?"

Because there was no other way that he could strike back at Gray, Blackwell said: "Go to hell, Jesse."

"Tell me about Davey!"

Blackwell grinned. "Go to hell," he said softly.

Gray leaped to his feet. He drew his gun and aimed it at Blackwell's belly.

"All right, Tom, you asked for it!" cried Gray, his mouth twisting.

The shot rang out, but there was no pain in Blackwell. He could not believe that Gray had missed at this close range. Then he saw that Gray's hat no longer was on his head. And as he watched, Jesse Gray crumpled under the impact of a second bullet. A moment later he lay sprawled out at Blackwell's feet . . . a bullet hole through his head.

Blackwell looked beyond Gray, and there, at the rim of the junipers, he saw Margarita Luz and Josélito. The Mexican said softly to the girl: "Miguel Gómez is avenged."

Chapter Eighteen

Blackwell rode up Triste Cañon, feeling more and more bitter and downhearted as the bay progressed. The reason for this was not clear to Blackwell. He did not know whether to attribute it to the melancholy desolation of the cañon, or to those events that had transpired recently.

He felt tired and worn. His joints ached, his muscles protested every move he made, the weariness seemed to have permeated even his soul. He would have given up the whole thing in despair had it not been for that one hope that still kept him going—Triste Cañon.

He kept remembering the last effort Luke Chandler had put out to utter those two words. They evidently meant something, but the importance of their meaning was a thing Blackwell could not conjecture. Perhaps this cañon had been Jesse Gray's hiding place. Dying, Chandler had realized he had not the time for explanation, so he had uttered the name of the cañon so that Blackwell could go there and find out for himself. If that were all, then this journey of Blackwell's was pointless and futile, for Jesse Gray was dead. On the other hand, this cañon might be the hiding place of the money, and it was this dim promise that had brought Blackwell here. But even if the money were hidden here, he could not hope to find it unless he knew the exact location. Triste Cañon was an awfully big place.

Blackwell had just about lost all hope when he came across the first sign that indicated the cañon had once been inhabited. On a small rise of ground he spotted the ruins of an old house and shed and several corrals. Sometime in the not too distant past someone had tried to run cattle in the forbidding confines of Triste Cañon, and these ruins existed as a mute memorial to his failure. Blackwell had seen a dry creek bed all the way up the canon, and he supposed that it had been the water in this now dry stream that had lured someone into trying his luck in this place. Then the creek had run dry and with it the hopes and expectations of that nameless someone who had been foolish or defiant enough to challenge the harshness of this land.

When Blackwell dismounted and looked into the ruins of the house, he saw signs of recent occupation. He was convinced that this had been Gray's hide-out, but still that did not put him any closer to the eight thousand dollars.

He stopped just outside the door and stared off at the bleakness of the cañon. Absently he reached in a shirt pocket for tobacco and papers, but then he saw something that arrested his movement. Far down the cañon, a mere speck in the distance, was a horseman.

Swiftly Blackwell reached for the lines of the bay and then led the horse around to the other side of the house where he would be out of sight of whoever was coming up the cañon. Peering around a corner of the ruined building, Blackwell patiently watched the coming of that rider.

It was Angel Dawson. She proceeded with a directness that indicated an old familiarity with this place. She paid no attention to the house. The girl rode straight to one of the old corrals. There she dismounted from her Arabian and immediately began digging at one of the corral posts.

There was coldness in Blackwell and the taste of gall in his mouth as he drew his gun and stepped out from behind the ruined house. The corral lay below him, at the foot of a small slope.

The girl was down on her knees as she dug in the ground. Her back was turned to Blackwell. At first, she was not aware of his approach for the earth was soft and the unyielding sand muffled the sound of his footsteps. Then Blackwell's spurs gave out a faint *jingle* when he was scarcely fifteen feet away, and this warned Angel Dawson.

She had found what she was looking for. As she jumped startled to her feet and whirled to face him, she was holding a pair of saddlebags. She fell back a step when she saw Blackwell. Her left hand rose for a moment to her throat, and she drew a deep breath, and then the astonishment left her and she was her old cool and haughty self again.

Blackwell took two more steps ahead and halted. "Hello, Angel," he said quietly, eyeing the saddlebags and then the .44 with the butt pointing forward at her left hip.

The girl's glance had dropped to Blackwell's gun. She stared at the weapon a moment, then those clear gray eyes lifted and studied Blackwell's face, as if trying to decide whether he would really use that gun.

"What's in those saddlebags, Angel?"

"Something that belongs to me."

"Why did you hide it 'way up here? Didn't you have any other place to put it?"

"I don't see where it's any of your business!"

"Is this where you live, Angel?"

"What if it is?"

"Someone has been living in that house," said Blackwell. "From the looks of it, I'd say it was a man. Jesse Gray."

She said nothing.

"Jesse told me things before he died," Blackwell said quietly, "everything . . . including the truth about you."

"That's a dirty lie," the girl snarled.

"Stop pretending, Angel," he said bitterly. "And hand over the saddlebags. I know the eight thousand's there. The roundup's finished, the tally book is closed. Jesse told me all about you. He thought he had me dead to rights, and he couldn't help bragging a little. Only Josélito showed up in time."

A look of defeat swept across Angel Dawson's face, indicating that she had seen Gray's body before riding to Triste Cañon and knew that the game was up.

"He told me how you'd come here to the Granadas to set everything up," Blackwell continued. "He told me how you worked on Sheppard and Hogarth. He told me why you came to me to try to get me to quit." His throat was dry. There was an ache in it. "I never really trusted you, Angel, and if you have any ideas that I'm going to be easy on you, forget them! You're the only living person who can clear Gómez's name, and you're riding to War Feather with me to tell Sheriff Richmond the truth."

After turning Angel Dawson over to the sheriff, Blackwell left War Feather and headed toward Margarita Luz's home. As he rode up to the door, he found Josélito about to take his leave. There was a reluctance about the big Mexican as he said his farewell.

"I have a feeling within me that we shall never meet again, *amigo,*" he said. "I also have a feeling that I have not long to live. But in whatever time is allotted me, I shall try to be a better man, I shall try to be a worthy man, because of you, *amigo.*"

Blackwell smiled. "I will always think well of you, Josélito."

Josélito put an arm around Blackwell's shoulders but this time the pressure was strangely and affectionately gentle. "And our Margarita?" asked the Mexican. "Is she not pretty?"

"I suppose she is. But what difference does it make how

she looks? It's what she is that matters. I've known prettier women than her but none as worthy or as fine as Margarita."

"Oh-ho?" said Josélito, grinning broadly. "Oh-ho? *¡Bueno!* I am most happy to hear you say this, *amigo*. Well, my friend," he said, his eyes reluctant and a little sad. "I must go. *¡Adiós!*"

"Vaya con Dios."

Blackwell watched Josélito until he was but a speck in the distance, then he turned to say good bye to Margarita Luz. But there was an indefinable quality about the girl that made him hesitate and appraise her in a new light. She in turn met his look without faltering, silently waiting for him to speak.

"Well, I guess I'd better be starting, too, Margarita."

"I know, Tom. I know you are eager to see your sister and your nephew, but why don't you rest here a few days first? It is a long trip for one who is tired and you have been through a lot since you arrived in the Granadas."

Blackwell did not need any urging. He spent three days at the ranch, helping Margarita Luz and riding with her. When the time finally came for him to ride back to Colorado, there was a strong unwillingness in him to leave the Granadas and Margarita Luz.

Although he had come to know her better in the last few days and recognized the depth of his feeling for her, he did not know what to make of her. He thought she cared for him, but she always appeared somewhat sad and forlorn, and he attributed this to her memory of Mike Gómez. Perhaps she was the kind who loved only once and thus her heart would remain with Gómez forever. This thought struck a small hurt and fear in Blackwell.

Still, he determined to have it out before he left, no matter how bitter and sorrowful the consequences might be. He said to her, bluntly and without preliminary: "Will you go to Colorado with me, Margarita? As my wife, I mean?"

She looked at him wonderingly for his face was so grave and hard. "Is the thought so distasteful to you," she asked, "that you most look so grim when you ask me that?"

"I'm not sure how you feel about Gómez," he said. "Maybe you don't want to have anyone else."

"I will always remember Mike. He was my first love, and I shall never forget him, but that does not mean I could never love anyone else." A tenderness came into her eyes as she looked at him. "I did not ask you to stay here only because you were tired, Tom."

A smile lighted his face. "Then you'll come? You'll come to Colorado with me?"

"When do we leave?" she asked.

The Longest Ride

Dixie was sitting in the rocker on the porch, smoking a cigarette, when I rode in. I turned the dun over to Curly. He asked me the old question with his eyes, but I pretended not to see. I started across the yard toward the house, and I looked once at the silvery white trailer sitting there to one side and sight of it almost made me wince. I turned my eyes quickly back to Dixie, hoping she hadn't noticed. If she had, she gave no sign. She just sat there, slowly rocking and smoking and watching me as I came up the steps.

I stopped and tried to hold her eyes, but I couldn't. My glance dropped to her legs, clothed in tight blue jeans, one knee crossed over the other while she sat and rocked.

"Any luck?" she asked.

My silence was her answer. After a while I looked up and found her staring off at the piñon-dotted hills. She drew deeply on her cigarette and blew the smoke out slowly. She did not look at me when she spoke.

"You were limping just now," she said. "You weren't limping early this morning."

"You know how it is. One minute I'm all right, and then the pain comes on all at once. I don't know what it is."

My eyes fell again, and I tried raising them and staring beyond her at the green and brown hills, but it was no go. All I saw was her small, round face topped with its head of short-cropped, blonde curls.

"We won't be going on the road until Monday," I said. "That gives me five days. I'll do it, Dixie. I can feel it in me. I'll do it by Monday."

"Will you?"

The chair creaked softly as she rocked. I felt sweat come out on my brow and on my neck. For a second I could have wept, but I got myself in hand and went inside.

In the kitchen I put the coffee pot on to boil. I got out a cigarette, but there was no taste to it, and after a couple of puffs I rubbed it out. I was standing there, listening to the faint throb of the pain in my thigh, when she came in.

"Would you like a cup, Dix?"

"No, thanks."

She went over to the tap and had a glass of water. I went up behind her and took her by the shoulders and turned her gently and pulled her near to me. She stood there quietly, almost resignedly. I bent my head and kissed her brow. It was smooth and cold.

"What's happening to us, Dix?"

"What do you mean?"

"It didn't used to be like this. Once it was something sweet and good. Now every day we seem to drift a little further apart."

She lifted her arms and pushed my hands off her shoulders, but she didn't move away. She stood there, reaching up to my chin, staring straight ahead at nothing.

"It's not unusual," she said. "We've been married a long time. Ten years, isn't it?"

"Right."

"Right? Oh. Well, anyway we're not newlyweds any more, Ben. We can't be smooching all the time. It's like that with everyone."

"But this is something more."

"Is it?"

She went over to the window that looked out on the pasture. Our horses were out there, the ones she used for trick riding and my string, the quarter horses I used for roping and bulldogging. They were all there, grazing. Curly sat on the top bar of the gate, watching them. He was the only hand we had, but he had nothing else to do.

I went over to Dixie. My right thigh twinged so fiercely once I had to clench my teeth. I had been all right that morning, as I'd been all right many mornings, but the pain always came back. I didn't want it to, but it always did. I could feel myself begin to sweat again.

"I'll be all right, Dixie," I told her. "I'll try again tomorrow morning. Maybe my leg will be all right then."

"There's nothing wrong with your leg."

My thigh twinged as if to mock her, but, of course, she couldn't feel the pain. Only I felt it, but of late I was beginning to wonder if that was what I was feeling.

"Things like these take time, Dix."

"You've had all summer and fall and winter since you were thrown in Cheyenne. The doctors all say your leg was mended perfectly. You have no trouble riding your saddlers."

"I told you I'm trying again in the morning. Something tells me that this time I'll do it."

She didn't say anything. She just went on staring out the window, watching the horses in the pasture. I put a hand on her arm and felt her tense as though something repulsive had touched her.

"I need you, Dix."

"For what? To hold you in the saddle so you won't be pitched off? You won't win any prize money that way."

"Please, Dix. Don't be like this."

"How do you want me to be?"

"Like in the old days."

"Then why don't you be like you were in the old days? The Ben Whitson I married . . . the Ben Whitson who rode Widow-Maker in Pendleton in 'Forty-Eight . . . the Ben

Whitson who was World's Champion Cowboy in 'Forty-Nine and 'Fifty. I'm not the only one who's changed."

I could feel the sweat gathering on my upper lip. There was something dry and aching in my throat. "I'll ride Big Red tomorrow. I promise you."

She swung around suddenly, and her eyes blazed up at me. "Why wait until tomorrow? You've still got all afternoon."

This time it was me who started watching the horses in the pasture.

"Do you want me to tell you how it will be tomorrow, Ben? Oh, you'll ride out to the old place, all right, and you'll probably saddle big Red. You've had all winter to gentle him so that now you can saddle him with no trouble at all. You'll do all of that."

I glanced at her, and the anger still burned in her eyes, anger and something more, something that made me feel low and shamed.

"But after you've saddled Big Red," she went on, "will you get up on him? I've been out there, Ben. I've ridden out there and watched from a distance. You always saddle Big Red, and then you just stand around, and after a while your leg starts to hurt."

"I need you, Dix, I need you to believe in me."

"The only thing you need is something you left up in Cheyenne."

I don't know what I'd have said to that, probably nothing. A car horn blasted outside right then, and Dixie crossed the kitchen and went outside. I followed her, a great hurt growing deeper and deeper inside of me.

It was Pat Gurney in his new convertible. Dixie went over and got in beside him. Gurney flashed me his white smile. He looked happy and prosperous, and he had every right to be. He'd had a good year, the one gone by.

"How's the boy, Ben?" he said. "Ride Big Red yet?"

I shook my head.

"Well, stick to it. You can do it. You're one of the best in the business."

"Thanks."

He looked at Dixie. She was staring straight ahead. Gurney brought his eyes back to me. They were bright with something that almost made me clench my fists.

"I'm taking Dixie to see some of the movies I made on the circuit. I caught Betty Faraday at Clovis last summer. She's tops. I figure Dixie might pick up a pointer or two from her and improve her act. Uh . . . do you mind, Ben?"

"Ben doesn't mind," Dixie said. She still hadn't turned her head.

Gurney gave a little laugh, low and awkward. Then he waved and put the convertible in gear. I watched until even the dust was gone. Then I went back into the kitchen, the pain in my thigh all forgotten. The coffee was burbling loudly. It made a lonesome sound.

The next morning Curly saddled the dun for me. I could have done it, but Curly insisted. He had so little to do it was more of a pastime for him. We kept Curly on because we had to have someone looking after the ranch while we were gone on the rodeo circuit.

I swung up into the saddle and settled myself. The leg felt fine this morning, but I knew enough not to hope for much.

" 'Luck, Ben," Curly said.

I looked down at him. He was lean and leathery, and the creases in his face were long and deep. The hair that showed under the brim of his Stetson was snow-white. He smiled encouragingly when he caught my eyes.

"You can do it, Ben," he said. "I went through it myself. I

know how it is, and I know it can be licked."

I looked around to see if Dixie had come outside. She was up, but I saw her nowhere, not even at one of the windows. I touched the dun lightly with a spur and headed up the road to the old place. When I topped the first rise, I hipped around in the saddle, hoping to see her now, but only Curly was there, watching me ride away. He waved an arm, and I waved in return, and then the dun was over the rise and going down the other side.

Big Red whinnied when he spotted me and the dun and came running over to the near side of the corral where he was penned. I had a lump of sugar for him, and he gobbled this. In the months that I'd been working on him he became somewhat of a pet, but he was still broncho. He still had not been ridden. I could see the devil in him in the clear of his eyes and in the rippling of the muscles in his front quarters and back and in the proud arching of his neck.

I had no trouble getting the saddle on him. I didn't even have to snub him to a post. I'd done this so often that I guess he was taking it as a game. He stood quietly with the blindfold over his eyes while I drew the cinches tight and slipped on the hackamore. Then he was ready. All I had to do now was step up into the saddle.

That was when the first twinge of pain came so sharply that I half shut my eyes. The palms of my hands grew wet. Something sick stirred in my belly. But Big Red stood there quietly, not even switching his tail, like a big gentle pony.

The twinge came again, and I pretended not to feel it. I heard Dixie now, those words echoing in my mind. *All you need is something you left up in Cheyenne.* I had almost cried, alone in my bed last night, remembering those words. I had almost crawled in shame

Dix, Dix, why don't you believe in me?

Big Red stirred a little, then quieted. It was always the same with him. Stand a while with the blindfold over his eyes and the saddle on his back and finally the saddle would come off and then the blindfold and the game would be over, for him.

I was sweating all over, sweat trickling down my cheeks, crawling down my sides and back and chest. The sickness was growing deeper in my belly, and I knew I would not hold out much longer. I heard those words again. *All you need is something you left in Cheyenne.*

I guess that's what did it, that and desperation. I grabbed the horn blindly and went up into the saddle with all the hurry I could muster. I felt Big Red shudder at this new part of the game and gather himself, and I almost threw myself off. But he quieted quickly and stood there very still under me, only his ears twitching.

I found the other stirrup with my right foot and settled it in place. I could hear the sound of my breathing, loud and ragged. The sweat still poured, my stomach still crawled.

I took the hackamore rope in my left hand, and with a right that trembled I reached forward slowly and took hold of the blindfold. The instant I touched it I almost let go, but her words echoed again.

"Dix." I said her name aloud this time, softly, and then I jerked the blindfold off.

I could feel Big Red tensing and setting himself, even though for a couple of seconds or so he moved not a muscle. Then he exploded. He snorted, a sound of puzzlement and fear and rage, and his back came up and his head jerked down, almost tearing the rope out of my hand, and with all four legs stiff as rods he went crow hopping around the corral.

I've no idea how long I stayed on. I don't even remember feeling any jolts. Big Red just took off, and all at once I was back in Cheyenne, sprawling in the dust, and above me that big black devil rearing high with his sharp forehoofs pawing the air and me underneath scrambling to get away, and those hoofs coming down, and then the pain and more pain, and I couldn't move and that black devil rearing above me again and the shouts of men and the squealing of horses and the pain and the blackness.

I found myself going out of the saddle, hitting the ground on the dead run and streaking for the bars of the corral and scrambling through. Big Red was going around in crazy little circles, trying to buck the saddle off.

I sat on the ground and put my face in my hands and wept. My whole body trembled and shuddered.

How long it was before I came out of it I don't know. I just looked up and around quickly, scared and ashamed, afraid that somebody had seen. I remembered what Dixie had said, and I scanned the piñon-mottled hills all around, searching, and, when I saw the rider coming in, I could have dug a hole and crawled into it.

The rider was a woman, but it wasn't Dixie.

I was standing and had brushed some of the dust from my pants when Laura Jean Masters rode up. She reined in her paint and looked down at me. I turned around and pretended to be staring at the old house and shack, the old place that Dixie and I had lived in before she had wanted a brand-new home.

Saddle leather squealed as Laura Jean dismounted. Her spurs tinkled softly as she walked over to me. I felt her touch my arm.

"Are you all right, Ben?"

"I suppose you saw?"

"Yes. Are you hurt anywhere?"

"Why don't you mind your own business?"

Her hand left my arm, and I was sorry for what I'd said, but I didn't tell her this. I didn't tell her anything. I just stared at the ground.

She moved around in front of me. I could see the small boots she wore and the wide, pale cuffs of her Levi's and the small, plain spurs.

"Look at me, Ben."

I kept staring at the ground.

"Look at me."

When I wouldn't raise my head, she grabbed my arms and shook me, and so I lifted my eyes. She had been a very pretty woman once, with long, shoulder-length auburn hair and clear hazel eyes, but that had been before that afternoon in Salinas. Now there were wrinkles in her brow and at the corners of her mouth and deep in her eyes a quick sadness.

"Why do you force yourself like this, Ben? You know it only makes it harder. Why do you drive yourself?"

"I've got to, Laura Jean. I've got to."

Her face moved past me for an instant as though she were thinking of something. Then it came back, and I had to wonder at how soft her eyes were and how long it was since Dixie had looked at me with eyes as soft.

"Are you going on the circuit?" she asked.

"Monday."

"You're not ready. Why don't you knock off for a year?"

"I can't."

She opened her mouth to say something, then changed her mind. Big Red had finally quit bucking and was scratching his rump against a corral post. She watched this a while, then her eyes returned to me. They seemed even sadder now. "It isn't only Big Red. It isn't only riding a bucking broncho again, is it?"

I said nothing.

"If it was only the riding part, it wouldn't be anything at all for you because you always were one of the best. But it's something more. Isn't it, Ben?"

Again I said nothing.

"You're trying it alone, but you can't do it alone."

I shrugged.

"Bob went through the same thing once," she said. Her eyes filmed as she remembered. "He wanted to try it alone because he wasn't sure how it would come out, and, if it came out bad for him, he didn't want anyone around to see. But he couldn't do it alone, and I didn't let him try more than twice. After that, I went with him. I watched him. I watched him get thrown several times, not because he couldn't stay on, but because he was afraid to stay on, but finally he licked it.

"I wanted him to quit then. We had our own place. I was tired of living half the year in a trailer, moving from town to town. But he wanted to prove to everybody he hadn't quit because he'd lost his courage. One more swing around the circuit, he told me. One more year to prove he had quit while he was still tops, and then we'd settle down and have the home and the children we'd always planned on. He was so happy to be back in it again because rodeoing was in his blood, and it was wonderful for both of us while it lasted."

She stopped now. Her teeth clamped down on her lower lip, and I knew she was thinking of the same thing I was, of that sunny afternoon in Salinas when Bob Masters took a bad fall. He'd busted some ribs and his lungs had been punctured and he'd died less than an hour later. I remembered because I'd been there that afternoon

I wanted to say something, but the right words just wouldn't come. So I put an arm around her shoulders and gave a little squeeze, and she buried her face against my shirt and stayed like that a while. I guess she cried a little, soundlessly, but she had rubbed her eyes dry by the time she looked up.

"Do you mind my coming over here and watching, Ben?" she asked. "I always worry that you might get hurt and there'd be no one around."

"No, Laura Jean," I told her. "I don't mind."

The next two days I rode out to the old place, but I didn't try to ride Big Red. I didn't even saddle him. I just saw to it that he had food and water, and then I sat around, watching him. When I grew tired of this, I mounted the dun and returned home.

That Saturday I finally knew what I wanted to do. It wasn't something that I'd just decided on, even though it had never come out quite so baldly in my mind any time before. It was the result of years of working and hoping and dreaming.

I caught Dixie putting the finishing touches on her lips, and I knew she was on her way to town. She gave me a quick look out of the corner of her eyes and saw instantly that nothing had happened. She picked up her bag and the keys to the pickup and started for the door.

"I want to talk to you, Dix."

She stopped. Her shoulders squared, but she didn't turn around. "What about?"

"Us."

She said nothing. She kept her back to me and stared straight ahead. I walked up behind her and started to put my hands on her arms, but I could sense her stiffen. I dropped my hands.

"Let's settle down, Dix."

"What do you mean?"

"We're not kids any more. I'm thirty-three and you're twenty-nine. We've got a pretty nice place here. We have a nice home. The ranch is all paid for. Let's settle down for good."

Her fingers gripped her bag so tightly the tips turned pale. "You mean quit rodeoing?"

"Yes."

"Why?"

"I just told you. I'm tired of knocking around. I've got this ranch paid for, and I'd like to start enjoying it."

"I see." She opened her bag and fished out a cigarette and lit it. She still had her back to me. "What will we live on?"

"You know I've always wanted to raise beef. That's the reason we bought this place, so I could go in the cattle business when I quit rodeoing."

She blew a cloud of smoke. "Where are you going to get the cattle? We don't own a single head."

"I plan on going down to Clovis next week and pick some up."

"How are you going to pay for them?"

"I know our bank balance is just about gone, but the ranch is clear. We can borrow on that."

She spun on her heel, eyes blazing. "And spend the rest of our lives paying off the mortgage?"

I could see it now. After all these years I could see how it really stood, but still in my mind I tried to deny it. "Please, Dix," I said. "If things break right for us, it shouldn't take too many years. The two of us together can do it. All I need is you to work with me. Like the old days."

"We don't have to mortgage one damn' little thing. All you have to do is have one good year on the circuit. We'd have enough money then to stock this place without having to borrow a single penny."

That finished me like a hard kick in the belly. That and the look in her eyes. When I didn't speak, she turned to leave.

"Where are you going?" I said.

She stopped, back stiffening. Again she would not look at me. "To see Pat Gurney."

My face clenched. "You've been seeing him a lot lately, haven't you?"

"So?"

"I don't like it."

"What're you going to do about it? Handle it the way you've handled Big Red?"

With that she left. She banged the front door shut, and soon after I heard the pickup start and leave the yard. Not until it shattered did I realize I had picked up a bottle off her dresser and hurled it at the far wall.

It was Saturday night, but I didn't go to town. She was there, most likely with Pat Gurney, and I didn't want to run into them together, and so I stayed home, in the darkness after night fell, staring into the shadows and remembering the good days that were no more.

After some time I switched on the lights and dug up a bottle of whisky and mixed several highballs, but they didn't help. Nothing helped any more.

Dix, Dix.

She wasn't home at midnight, and so I undressed and turned off the lights and went to bed. I don't know how long I lay there, trying to sleep, able only to think of that other bed standing there empty.

Finally she returned. I heard the pickup enter the yard and then her footsteps in the house. She did not switch on the lights of our room, only the bathroom. Through the half open doorway I could see her shadow as she moved about. After a while she turned the light off. I was standing, waiting for her, when she came over to get in her bed.

"I'm sorry, Dix," I said, putting myself in front of her so

she could not get by me. "I'm sorry about this afternoon. I'll go on the circuit. Just one more year. We'll have all the things I've always promised you. Just wait and see."

There was only silence when I stopped talking, silence and the scent of peach blossoms and her nearness.

"I'll be all right," I told her. I was beginning to sweat. "I'll just have to get into it gradually. I'll let the riding events go at first. But I'll enter the bulldogging and the roping. After I get the feel of things, I'm sure the riding will come back."

"You were always strongest in the riding events. You were always a cinch for some prize money there. You never did make much at bulldogging and roping."

"But I'll ride. Just give me time." I crawled now. It shamed and sickened me, but I crawled. I wanted to keep her that bad. "Please, Dix. I'll do anything for you, anything you say. Please don't let me lose you."

I started to reach for her, but she laughed and pushed me away. She didn't push hard enough to stop me. It was the laugh that stopped me, the scorn and the contempt in it. She brushed past me, and I heard the rustle of sheets as she got in between them and I knew she was lying there with her back turned toward me. I stood there, crying silently inside, remembering all those old days and nights, and knowing a loneliness I'd never felt before.

Sunday morning the sky was gray. A cold and bitter wind blew across the piñon-marked hills, and up on the high peaks it was snowing. I was going to go out and take a look at Big Red, but I didn't feel up to it. I took the pickup, instead, and went to town for the Sunday papers.

On the way back I was just turning off the road into our gate when I saw the station wagon coming. It was Laura Jean Masters. She tooted her horn, and so I stopped and got out.

She pulled over and rolled down her window. I saw her eyes searching my face, asking the inevitable question, and I looked beyond her and said: "Not yet, Laura Jean. I haven't even tried since that day."

"You still going on the road tomorrow?"

I nodded.

"Why?"

"I've got no choice. Rodeoing is all I know."

She didn't say anything right away. I could feel her studying my face, but I wouldn't look at her. I kept staring off at the distant hills, but I wasn't seeing them. I was seeing something else.

After a while she said: "It's Dixie, isn't it?"

I swung my head and stared at her, hard.

"I know it isn't any of my business, Ben, but she's no good for you. She's never been. She's selfish and. . . . Well, she's just not good for you."

"I love her, Laura Jean."

She showed a small, wan smile. "Yes, I know. That's the sad part of it."

"It's for only one more year, to get some money so we can stock the ranch. That's the only way I know to earn that money. After this year I quit for good."

"Do you really believe that?"

I said nothing.

She reached out the window and touched my arm. "Look, Ben, let's stop kidding ourselves. You know Dixie better than I do. You know the way she likes to live. Do you really believe she'll ever change? She's used to being the wife of one of the top men in rodeoing. She'll break your heart, Ben, if she hasn't broken it already. Oh, you'll be left with some beautiful memories, but they'll never be enough. I know. I've got some beautiful memories. I'll always have them. They're the only thing I have to take to bed with me at night. Is that what you take to bed with you? Memories?"

I turned away swiftly and blindly. I jumped in the pickup and started it. Behind me she was crying: "Ben, Ben. Please. I didn't mean it that way, Ben."

But I wasn't heeding her. I wasn't heeding anything. I got that pickup under way, and I went down that road with the gas pedal all the way to the floor. Sometimes I hardly saw, but I was able to stay on the road and storm through the yard and take the way to the old place.

I had to slow down here, but I didn't slow much. We always used horses or the jeep to go to the old place, the road was that bad. We'd never used the pickup before, but I used it now. I used it, and I didn't care if I tore the bottom out of it.

I don't remember much of it, I was that mad and hurt. I saddled Big Red and got up on him. I remember him squealing and snorting and rearing and crow hopping and sunfishing. I remember once he reared so high I thought he was going over backward, but I didn't quit the saddle. I just took the hard, knotted end of the hackamore rope and swatted him over the nose with it, and he screamed but he went down on all four hoofs again. I remember choking dust and teeth-cracking jolts and the taste of blood in my mouth.

Then it was over. Big Red wasn't pitching any more. He was just standing there on widespread, shivering legs and under me his big barrel heaved while the breath whistled out of his nostrils. I got down. I was still mad and hurt.

Even if Gurney hadn't been there, it wouldn't have made any difference. I had already decided on what I was going to do. Finding Gurney there only made it easier.

He was on the porch with Dixie, and, the instant I stepped out of the pickup they knew I had finally done it. My clothes showed it. They were wet with sweat and covered with dust. I'd lost my hat back there in the corral with Big Red and forgotten to pick it up. They watched me as I mounted the steps, and the mockery went out of Gurney's face when he caught my eyes.

I didn't give either of them a chance to say a word. Gurney saw it coming, and he threw up his fists, but that was only a feint with me. I slammed him in the groin as hard as I could with my knee, and, when he doubled up, I clipped him on the jaw and sent him sprawling down the steps into the dirt of the yard. He stayed there, too, twisted up in a knot, groaning and retching.

Then I turned on Dixie. Her face had paled. Fright made her eyes big and luminous but they didn't move me any more. "Get out," I told her. "Never let me set eyes on either one of you again."

That evening I drove over to Laura Jean's place. She heard my jeep and came outside. One look at my face and she knew I'd succeeded with Big Red.

"I saw your pickup and trailer going by less than an hour ago," she said.

"That was Dixie. I told her I didn't ever want to set eyes on her again."

"Then you aren't going on the road tomorrow?"

I took her chin in my thumb and forefinger and tilted her head so that I could look down into those soft, hazel eyes. "Tomorrow I'm going to the bank and arranging credit. Then I'm going to Clovis and buy some stock. It'll take several hard years, Laura Jean, years of working and saving, but I know I can do it with the right one. It'll take a little while to get free of Dixie. Would you wait that long?"

Two tears formed in her eyes and trickled down her cheeks, but she was smiling, and it was a happy smile. "I don't mind, Ben," she said. "I don't mind at all when I've got something to wait for."

A Time for Rifles

The lights that they were to use later were in a tackle box. Caldwell placed the box in the trunk of the car beside the rifles that were covered with a blanket. He could feel Bridgeman watching. And when Caldwell glanced at him, Bridgeman smiled—the tight, secretive smile that evinced as little emotion as the opaque look in his gray eyes.

"All set?" Bridgeman asked.

Caldwell nodded. Bridgeman's wife didn't even nod.

The three of them sat in the front seat. Behind them, on the floor, were the bait bucket and another tackle box and three fishing rods, things that they would not use. The car knifed without too much sound through the soft summer night.

Rae Bridgeman sat quietly between the two men. Caldwell was very much aware of her nearness. It started that strong something to running through him, the something that disturbed and upset him and made him think of the loaded rifles in the trunk of the car and of the dark purpose that had come to live with him since the night he had held her in his arms.

It was almost as though she were thinking of the same thing, for he felt her shudder. Her voice came soft and small, like a little girl's, and this was not at all like her.

"Is it worth it, dear?" she asked Bridgeman. "The risk, I mean? They hand out stiff fines for shining deer, especially if you're from down state."

Bridgeman laughed, light and easy. Caldwell glanced at him, but could not read the look on Bridgeman's face, not by the dim light of the dashboard.

"Relax, hon. Me and Joe are old hands at this, aren't we,

Joe? Remember the old days, before I moved to the city? We were young punks then, and we did our share of violating. Isn't that right?"

Caldwell glanced out the window, at the black, inscrutable face of the forest whipping by. The headlights picked up the goldenrod and thistles that grew tall on either side of the brown road.

"Yes, we knocked off a few deer," Caldwell said.

He felt Rae's glance switch to him, but he would not look at her.

"I've heard Lew talk about it," she said, "but that was just out of season. You never did any shining, did you, Joe?"

"No."

"Why are you doing it now, then?"

Caldwell said nothing.

Bridgeman laughed, soft and without emotion.

Doesn't he suspect? Caldwell's thought was angry. *Doesn't he have any idea at all? Is it going to be as simple as hitting a target?*

"I want to take some venison back, hon," Bridgeman said. "The deer are nice and fat now. And they taste much better out of season. Don't they, Joe?"

Caldwell grunted and went on staring out of the window. He felt Rae stir beside him.

"Oh, you two," she said, and made a sound of disgust. "You seem to think it's just a game."

"It is," Bridgeman said. "A game between us and the wardens. We always were smarter than them."

"Why don't you just shoot deer when it's . . . it's daylight?" Rae asked, still exasperated. "Why shine them?"

"It's easier that way, that's why," Bridgeman said. The flat, toneless laugh followed the statement. It was starting to get on Caldwell's nerves. "A deer'll freeze when you get him in the light, just stand there with his eyes reflecting the light. So you can shoot him right between the eyes. Now you know. What's more, there are no wardens out after midnight, unless they've been tipped off."

"I hope you're right," Rae said.

"Nag, nag," Bridgeman said, teasing.

Rae said nothing. She settled deeper into the seat and stared straight ahead, lost in thought.

The car sped on. There was no traffic on this lonely road. The headlights picked up nothing but the curves and undulations of the brown road and the silent stand of the timber on either side.

Caldwell opened the trunk and took the lights out of the tackle box and handed one to Bridgeman. Then he took the loaded rifles out from under the blanket. He thought his hand would tremble, but it was steady as he handed a gun to Bridgeman. There was a third gun, a carbine, in the trunk.

"Do you want yours?" Caldwell asked Rae.

"Take it," Bridgeman said when Rae hesitated. "It might make you feel better."

"Are you taking her with you?" Caldwell asked. He felt his throat tighten as he spoke and his heart falter and skip a beat.

"Not unless she wants to come," Bridgeman said. "Do you, hon?"

Her eyes searched them both, briefly.

Has she seen something? Caldwell thought. *Has she guessed?* But her guessing was not so important as Bridgeman's. He was the one who must not guess.

"No," she said in that strange, small voice. "I can stay here in the car."

"Take the gun," Bridgeman said again.

"Why?"

"A deer might come along."

"I wouldn't know what to do if one did."

"All you gotta do is turn the headlights on. That'll stop him and then you can shoot him. You won't miss. You're a good shot. I know because I taught you."

Still she hesitated.

Bridgeman shrugged. "All right, then. I just thought the gun'd make you feel better, being left here alone."

"OK," Rae said. "I'll take it."

Her hand brushed Caldwell's as he gave her the carbine. Her fingers were ice cold and seemed to linger a moment against his. Was she trying to tell him something? Reassure him? He had not told her anything, but she might have guessed. He had wanted to tell her, but had not known how to put it into words. Maybe she did know and was comforting him with that touch. It should have made him experience relief. Instead, he tightened up still more and felt sweat bead his brow.

"What's the matter with you?"

Bridgeman's sudden question caused Caldwell to start. But he forced his voice to be calm and expressionless. "Nothing. Why?"

"You don't seem so enthusiastic about this trip any more. You've hardly said a word all night."

"I've been thinking. It'll go rough on us if we're caught."

"Well, it was as much your idea as mine," Bridgeman said.

He peered harder, but Caldwell was sure Bridgeman could see nothing on his face in the dark even if something were there. Still, it made him uneasy with Bridgeman staring like that.

"You want to call it off?" Bridgeman asked.

"No." He said it quickly—almost too quickly. He had to get himself in hand. He had to stop letting his imagination run away from him. Bridgeman knew nothing and guessed nothing, and in a short while now it would be over. He drew a deep breath, careful not to make it audible. "Well, let's get started."

"You said to carry the light at the waist?" Bridgeman asked.

They were mining lights that Caldwell had taken from the iron ore mine where he worked. There they wore the lamps on their hats, but this was not mining. And it was certainly more deadly than mining with what he had in mind.

"Yes," Caldwell said. "That way both your hands are free to use the rifle."

He watched Bridgeman clip the lamp in place. In the silence he could hear the sound of his own breathing and the soft sound of Rae stirring. She stood on tiptoe and kissed Bridgeman.

"Be careful, dear," she said.

"Don't get scared if you hear several shots," Bridgeman said. "We'll be back."

"So long, Joe," Rae said.

"So long," Caldwell answered.

Then he and Bridgeman were moving off, up the road, the scuffing of their heavy shoes on the road the only break in the vast and solemn silence of the forest.

He remembered the spot, whereas Bridgeman didn't, because Bridgeman had been away for several years while he had hunted and fished in this country without interruption. Bridgeman would have passed up the place. It was Caldwell who stopped, and Bridgeman, aware that he had, turned and came back a few steps.

Bridgeman glanced about, at the unfamiliar pattern of trees and brush standing stark and stolid in the bright moonlight. "Is this the deer run?" he asked.

"Don't you remember?"

"There's a lot more brush." Bridgeman peered at the second-growth timber that had taken over this cutover land. "But I remember now."

Caldwell was aware of the quickened beating of his heart. *Why don't I just let him have it here and now?* he thought with a touch of panic. *Why not get it over with? He'll be just as dead.*

Then Caldwell got himself in hand. It had to look like an accident and so it could not be done here, not on the open road.

"Well, take your pick," he said, noting that his voice had turned thick and gruff.

Bridgeman stared at him.

"Which side do you want?" Caldwell said, fighting a strong impatience. "You take the deer run on one side of the road, and I'll take the other."

Bridgeman went on staring, not saying anything. There seemed to be something cold and calculating in his silent immobility, and Caldwell told himself to stop imagining things.

"How far do you want me to go?" Bridgeman finally asked.

"Not too far. Just so it's a ways off the road. We don't want to kill anything too close to the road, but not too far, either." He could feel himself start to sweat again. "We won't have to carry anything too far that way."

Have I fooled you? he thought with the flutter of apprehension and panic in his stomach. *Or do you know? Is that why you're looking at me like that? But how can you know?*

Then Bridgeman smiled. Caldwell could see the flash of his teeth in the moonlight. "Well, 'luck, Joe," Bridgeman said.

" 'Luck, Lew."

He dropped to one knee and pretended to tie his shoelace

while Bridgeman crossed to the far side of the road. He did not want to present his back to the other. As Bridgeman crossed the ditch with one long stride, Caldwell straightened and ducked into the brush. A branch lashed his cheek and scratched it. Then he was through the clumps and out of sight, and there he stopped, listening to the drumming of his heart and the repetitions of self-reproach.

He had to wait. He could not follow too soon. He had to let some time elapse. Then he could say he had followed a deer across the road and had shot at the deer. This was the story he had decided on. So he had to wait, with patience, although patience was something that he now found most difficult. Still he waited, all on edge, dreading, but he wanted her so much.

Rae.

She came before his eyes now, beautiful, desirable. He had sensed the thing begin in him the first time he had seen her. He had fought against it then, because he and Lew Bridgeman had grown up together and had been friends. But she had never resented his attentions and she had told him the first time they'd been alone that she wasn't very happy and in that moment the purpose had been born, and so here he was, holding a rifle in dampened hands, waiting, waiting.

He brushed a hand across his eyes and forehead, and the fingers came away wet. He had to put her from his mind, he told himself. He had to concentrate all his thinking on what lay ahead, what must be done. He could not be sure that Bridgeman had not guessed and was there across the road, waiting, too.

He drew a deep breath and told himself he did not have to be foolishly direct and open about it. He would go farther up the road, under cover of the brush, until he was over the rise, and there he would cross and, even if Bridgeman were waiting, he would come up on him from behind.

This plan took some of the edginess from him. The sweating eased, the beating of his heart softened. In a little while he felt quite calm and objective about what he was going to do.

He parted the brush and looked across the road where Bridgeman had disappeared. The blank face of the forest stared back at him. He glanced up and down the road, visible in the moonlight, and he was just in time to catch sight of someone slim and slight enter the timber on his side of the fire-line.

Rae. Rae.

It was several moments before he could begin to think. *So she had a reason for not coming with them, for pretending reluctance in accepting the carbine. What was it?*

There were several answers, and this complexity all but drove him frantic. Maybe she and Bridgeman were in this together, maybe that was how she had schemed to escape Bridgeman's wrath, by helping him kill her lover. Or maybe Bridgeman didn't know, and she was out to kill Caldwell before he could tell about the two of them. Or maybe—wildly, now—there was someone else, and she saw in this situation an opportunity of getting rid of both him and Bridgeman. Or maybe she really loved him and was coming to tell him so and to warn him and to help him.

Rae. He almost sobbed the name. *Rae. How can I be sure of you? How can I be sure of anything?*

He turned and stared along the deer run. The brush lessened as he drew away from the road and soon disappeared. Here the trees, rough and stately, stood like pillars of a vast temple, and the ground beneath was clear of underbrush. Moonlight filtered through intertwining branches and here and there laid fragile patterns on the floor of the forest.

The deer run was a definite trail through the timber, and Caldwell went along it quite easily.

After a while, when his breath had quickened from the pace of his walking, he halted. He took the lamp, which he had left unlit, and hung it and the battery on a low limb. He switched the light on and then went to one side, away from the glow, and stood and waited with his back against the bole of an oak.

His straining ears picked up sounds arising out of the stillness of the forest, many of which he credited to his imagination. The lamp, swinging a little on the branch, gave out a winking glow. Sweat lay hot and sticky on him.

Although he was waiting for it, the shot, when it came, made him jump. The bullet smashed into the orb of the lamp, snuffing out the light instantly, and then went shrieking down the avenues of the trees. The echoes rolled back and forth, fading into silence.

He got down on one knee and waited, his heart beating hard and heavy. Righteous anger came, and then hate. *I'm in the driver's seat now,* he thought. *If you want to come and make sure you've hit me, I'm here waiting. You'll want to do that, won't you, Rae? You'll want to make sure. Well, come on, then. I'm here to welcome you.*

He gripped the rifle so hard, he felt his fingertips sting as the circulation was cut off. So he drew a breath and forced some of the tenseness from him and went on waiting.

Finally he spied a flicker there ahead of him, a faint winking of a light as someone moved in on him. A sudden burst of rage made him whip the rifle to his shoulder and aim at the approaching glow. Then his finger remained motionless on the trigger, as the thought came that this might be Bridgeman, after all. He had to know first; he had to be sure. The killing could come afterward.

He moved in a small circle, going silently through the trees, the oncoming glow a beacon to guide him. Whoever it was seemed pretty sure the bullet had done its work, for the approach was direct and open. Twigs snapped underfoot and old, wet leaves made soft, mulching sounds. Caldwell moved in behind the walking figure and with a swift step got up close and shoved the barrel of the rifle harshly against its back.

A shrill, startled voice cried out and then was abruptly still. He saw the figure sag and crumple to its knees, and in that moment of recognition he did not know which he preferred—being there alive, looking down at the frightened, sobbing woman, or lying dead among last year's spoor.

He picked up the flashlight from where it had fallen from her hand and switched the glow off. She was still down on her knees, making great, gasping sounds of either vast exhaustion or near hysteria. He picked the carbine up, too, and stood there, holding a gun in either hand

After a while she looked up at him. He could see the pale blob of her face. He imagined it would be beautiful if he could see it clearly and very concerned and very tragic. But it moved him even less than would a stranger's photograph on a wall.

"Joe?" Her voice came small and quavering and uncertain. "Is that you, Joe?"

He said nothing. He stood and stared mutely down at her.

"Are you all right? I heard the shot. I feared so much for you. He's out to kill you, Joe. But you know that now. Are you sure you're all right?"

He stood and listened to the voice of disenchantment. *To think I would have killed for you,* he said to himself. All at once he envied animals that burrow, for he would have liked to crawl deep into the earth, never to emerge.

She turned so that she faced him squarely, her head uplifted and hands outstretched, like some supplicating Madonna. "Joe? Aren't you going to say something, Joe?"

"What is there to say?" His voice sounded thick and harsh, a stranger's voice.

She reached a hand out to touch him, and he drew back sharply. The movement was a revelation to her of all he thought, and she made a sound, half of disbelief, half of pain.

"Joe! You don't think I . . . ? You can't think it was me who . . . who shot at you?"

"I suppose it was *him,*" he said. "How dumb do you think I am?"

"Oh, Joe, Joe. How can you think a thing like that of me? I came to warn you. I never had a chance to before. He was always with us. That's why I pretended to stay in the car, but I followed, so I could come and tell you. He hates you. He hasn't said a word about it, but I know him and his ways, and he hates you very much and means to kill you. Don't you believe me?"

Another time he might have, he thought, before he had glimpsed her rottenness, and his own. He wondered which was the more vile, hers or his.

"Joe." She was crying openly now. "I never thought you'd have so little faith in me. Go on. Why don't you look at my gun? That will tell you if I shot at you. . . ."

They huddled in the darkness. He put an arm about her, and she rested her face on his shoulder. She wept silently, giving voice to sorrow and hurt and bewilderment.

He wanted to tell her—after having examined the carbine and finding it fully loaded and unfired—*I'm sorry, Rae. I'm really very sorry. It's just that I'm all mixed up. I want you so much I thought I could kill to try to get you. Please forgive me.* The words were fully formed in his mind, but somehow he could not pronounce them.

Her sobs finally stilled; she looked up at him. "Do you think he's still out there?" she whispered.

His answer was a whisper, too. "I don't know."

"What are we going to do?"

He had been asking himself the same thing without finding an answer. "Stay here, I guess.

He felt her shiver. "You mean . . . just wait for him?"

"The way I see it, he has to wait, too. He's not sure he hit me when he fired. He's not even sure he smashed my light. For all he knows, I just switched it off. That's why he won't come looking. He can't take the chance of stumbling into me. So he'll have to wait, too."

"Couldn't we leave? Couldn't we go back to the car?"

"And run into him on the way?"

"We could circle, couldn't we? And come out on the road. You know this country."

"That's where he's probably waiting. On the road. Between us and the car. No, Rae. We've got to wait."

"For how long?"

To that he had no answer.

"Until morning?" she asked.

"In daylight I'll make a better target," he said grimly.

She put her face in her hands, so that the sound of her sobbing would not carry far. "It's all my fault. If I wasn't such an awful person, this never would have happened."

He stroked her hair, the silken hair, and knew sadness and regret. "Don't cry, Rae. It's more my fault than yours. Don't cry."

"I'm promiscuous."

"No. No, you're not."

"I am. And that's a nice word for it. There've been others besides you. Lew and I made a poor marriage, but he won't call it quits. He says I'm just upset because we can't have children. He won't do anything to give me cause to divorce him. He's been hurt before, but he did nothing about the others. You're the only one he's tried to kill. You, the one who means something to me. The others never meant anything."

"That's because he knows I meant to kill him," Caldwell said, for a moment knowing sympathy rather than hate. "In one way I don't blame him."

"Maybe if I talked to him."

He stared at her. She had stopped crying. She was looking up at him rather solemnly, her face pale and sad in the shadows.

"I'll go to him," she said. "I'll talk him out of it. I'll promise to be good to him from now on. He'll listen to me because he loves me."

"No."

"Why not? It's you he wants to kill."

He shook his head in bewilderment. Something told him that this was wrong, the irreparable error. But he did not know why it was. "He might not recognize you," he said.

"I'll be careful. I'll call to him first."

He shook his head again. He knew now it was the thought of losing her for good that hurt him.

She kissed him softly. Her lips felt cold and stiff. "I love you. Always remember that, Joe. You're the one I really love. Will you remember?"

"I don't want you to go." He thought the anguish would show in his voice, but his tone was flat. "I'll figure something out."

"No, my darling. I don't want you dead and, strangely, I don't want him dead, either. I want you both to live. Mine is the only way. After all, I started this. It's only right that I finish it."

"I won't be able to see you again?" The pain that he felt was in his voice now.

"No, Joe. This is good bye."

He held her tightly and kissed her fiercely, and he supposed there were tears because his eyes stung, and then she was going, walking away from him down the avenues of the trees, in sight for a few brief moments, and then gone.

He stood in loneliness and sorrow. All his mind could hold was the thought that she was gone. She had taken the carbine and the flashlight with her, and all he had left to remember her by was an image in memory.

He wanted to cry out, to call her back, but it was too late. She should almost be there by now. It was then that the realization struck him with all its horror and in that same instant the shot came.

He walked with dull, unhurried steps, for what had happened was already done, and he would not allow himself the loophole of hope. So there was no need to hurry. He made his slow way through the trees and even stopped to disengage a branch that caught in the cloth of his jacket, and then he stepped through the brush and out into the clear moonlight that washed the road.

Bridgeman had picked her up and carried her out of the woods and laid her on her back on the road. He was down on his knees beside her. He looked up as Caldwell walked in, rifle cocked and ready at his hip.

She lay in that utter quietness that is the mark of death. She still clutched the shattered flashlight that she had held against her heart to guide the bullet.

Bridgeman lifted pleading hands to Caldwell. "Kill me. Go ahead, kill me. You think I want to live with this on my mind?"

Caldwell lifted the rifle and aimed it. He was cold and grim inside, and detached, as though another Joe Caldwell stood on the side and watched like a spectator of a play.

"What are you waiting for?" Bridgeman cried, tears streaming down his face. "I killed her, didn't I? I thought it was you I was killing. She didn't make a sound. She didn't even answer when I called out. All I saw was the light, and I shot at it. Damn you, Joe, aren't you going to kill me?"

Caldwell heard other words, as he knew he would forever hear them. *I want you both to live. Mine is the only way. After all, I started this.* The rifle fell, and he turned away and stared at the watching, brooding forest.

Why? he asked mutely. *Why like this? Why?*

The forest held its silence.

Look for the Blue Roan

He was young and, until now, very proud of his deputy star. He had run in drunks on Saturday nights and he'd made arrests for disturbing the peace and for vagrancy and he'd gone through the county tacking notices of auctions and circuit court meetings on fence posts and barns. For three months he had done these things efficiently and impersonally, as befitted a man with his job and responsibility. The feelings of his heart had never modified his sense of duty, but this job was something different.

He rode into the yard of Twin Bells, feeling very much ill at ease. The warrant, which was folded and buttoned securely in his shirt pocket, seemed to rest there with an enormous, depressing weight. He was aware of hardly anything else, only this unpleasantness, but he told himself this was his job and he should never have got into it if he was going to let it affect him like this. So he tightened his lips and shrugged the reluctance away and dismounted.

He stood a while beside his sorrel, looking about him. He made a show of stretching and limbering up as if the ride here to Twin Bells had tired him, but it was only pretense. It helped to make more time pass before he served the warrant.

Twin Bells was a tiny ranch that lay at the foot of the mountain. Today there was a strong wind boring down the heights, carrying with it the resinous smell of pines. The ranch yard seemed deserted. The corrals were empty, and the windmill clanked furiously in the wind.

Deputy Johnny Hull cursed silently and walked up to the door of the house. He was about to knock when it opened and the girl stood there. She had on a little print dress and a white apron, and her arms were bare and wet as if she had been doing dishes. She regarded him as from a distance, arch and cool.

"Yes?" she said.

He'd had a couple of waltzes with her at the dance two Saturdays ago. He had asked to see her home, but she had demurred. For two weeks he had tried to think up some excuse for coming around to Twin Bells. Now he had it—but it was a reason, not an excuse.

"Is your brother home?" He thought he sounded cold and impersonal.

She had hair the color of bronze. Sun slanted in and struck sparks out of it. A strand drifted across her cheek. She brushed it back with a wet hand.

"What do you want with him?" Her eyes were fixed on his deputy's star.

Her glance made him uncomfortable. The star pinned to his shirt seemed to take on a ponderous weight. It was almost like a wall between them.

"I just want to see him, that's all." He was trying to make it sound casual and unimportant.

Her eyes narrowed slightly. "Is it on business?"

"You could call it that."

"My brother isn't in right now, Mister Hull," she said smoothly. "I don't expect him home until evening. When he comes in, I'll tell him about you, and, if it's anything important, he'll ride right on to Arrowhead."

"I'll wait," said Johnny Hull. "Maybe he'll come home early."

The girl shrugged, too quickly, too nonchalantly. "If you want to waste your time," she said. She was eyeing him with a studied interest. "How important is your business with Wade?"

Johnny Hull thought of the warrant in his pocket and of how anxious she seemed that he ride on and of the blue roan in the corral, and it all added up to something that made him feel mean and miserable. But this was a deputy's job. The sheriff was laid up with a broken leg and so all the dirty tasks fell to him. It was all in the day's work.

Johnny Hull's jaw set stubbornly. "Important enough for me to hang around until he comes home."

"Well, if you don't have anything better to do," she snapped, and slammed the door in Johnny Hull's face.

He stepped back and walked over to his sorrel, flushing with anger and mortification. This experience was a world apart from what he had once dreamed his first visit to Twin Bells would be like. He had never figured that the visit would be undertaken in an official capacity. Now he was here, and, if he had never gotten off on the wrong foot before, he had now with Kate Gilbert.

He fussed with the sorrel's mane and then checked the cinch, killing time while he decided what to do. He had a warrant, and he believed he had the right to force his way into the house for a search. But when he looked at the house, that closed door seemed to stare back at him mockingly.

Irritation and anger rose in Johnny Hull. He took out tobacco and papers and built a smoke, but, when he had lighted it, he found he didn't want it. He ground the unsmoked cigarette under his toe and silently cursed.

Squatting on his toes, he began to trace aimless patterns in the dust. He glanced once at the house, but the door remained closed. He stared a while at the corral, watching the blue roan pacing restlessly about the enclosure. Then another sound came from the barn.

Johnny Hull glanced that way, and what he saw made him rise hurriedly to his feet. Someone had come out of the barn and was walking toward him. It was Wade Gilbert.

There was a sheepish look on Wade Gilbert's round, good-natured face. His eyes kept wandering from Johnny Hull's, and he seemed unable to decide what to do with his hands, whether to keep them in his pockets or out.

"Hello, Johnny," he said. "Been here long? I was kind of busy and didn't hear you ride up."

Johnny Hull didn't say anything. He saw how it was. At first, Gilbert had decided to bluff it out, to remain in hiding in the barn somewhere. Then he must have thought it over and had concluded it was best if he faced the music. This and the blue roan added up to nothing good. Johnny Hull felt a little sad about it.

When he didn't speak, Gilbert said: "Something you want, Johnny?"

Hull took the warrant out of his pocket. "I've got to arrest you, Wade."

Gilbert didn't take the paper. He waved it away. "Arrest me?" he cried, trying to sound surprised and indignant. "What for?"

"That stage hold-up on the Fort Benson road three days ago."

"I didn't do it."

"That's not for me to decide," said Johnny Hull. "My job is to take you in to Arrowhead for a hearing." He looked at Wade Gilbert's gunless waist, then lifted his glance to Gilbert's face. It looked sick but not defiant.

"You coming, Wade?" Hull asked gently.

"I didn't do it," Gilbert said tonelessly, a whipped look in his eyes.

"You'll have a chance to tell your side if it."

"Sure," said Gilbert. "Sure." His head bowed as if he were going over the whole thing in his mind. He scuffed dirt morosely with the toe of a boot. Finally he said: “I’ll saddle a horse.”

“Take the blue roan,” said Hull.

Gilbert’s head lifted sharply, and for an instant defiance made his eyes bright. “So that’s it,” he muttered. “I’m the only one in the county who owns a blue roan now.”

Hull shrugged. “I got my orders.”

The blue roan whinnied as Gilbert approached the corral. The horse was like a pet, Johnny Hull thought, and he could understand how Wade Gilbert must feel. While Gilbert was saddling, Hull stared disgustedly at the ground.

His back was to the house, and he heard the door open, but he didn’t turn. Then something warned him, and he jumped aside just in time. The dishwater splashed the ground where he had been standing a moment before.

Johnny whirled, face flushing with helpless anger, to see Kate Gilbert with the empty dishpan in her hands. Her nose went up in the air as his eyes fell on her, and she started archly away.

“You watch what you’re doing,” he growled at her.

“Why don’t you arrest me, too?” she snapped.

Gilbert had the roan saddled and was leading the horse over to Hull. He tried to put on a smile as his sister reached him. She was tense and angry.

“You know it’s a frame-up, Wade,” she said in a low, wrathful tone. “As soon as we heard the bandit rode a blue roan, we knew what to expect. I told you to run for it!”

Gilbert spread his hands in a helpless posture. “If I’d run, I’d’ve admitted I was guilty. I’ve got no choice, Kate. I’ve got to face the music and make them see how it really was.” He patted her shoulder. “I’ll be all right.”

“Wait a minute,” she said, turning away. “I’m riding to Arrowhead, too.”

"No. I'll be all right. I'll bet I'll be home for supper, won't I, Johnny?"

Johnny Hull shrugged and said nothing. He was sorry he had ever pinned on a deputy's star.

Wade Gilbert swung up on the blue roan, and Hull mounted his sorrel. Gilbert smiled at his sister and lifted a hand in farewell, and then spurred down the trail.

Johnny Hull followed. He was conscious of Kate Gilbert, standing there, watching them go from sight, but, although the urge was strong in him, he never once turned to look back.

They were gathered in the county prosecutor's office on the second floor of the courthouse in Arrowhead. Deputy Johnny Hull and his prisoner, Wade Gilbert, Emory Taylor, who had been the driver on the Fort Benson stage, and the gun guard, Rush McErvain, and the prosecutor, Sam Russell.

Russell was saying to Taylor and McErvain: "Well, you've seen the blue roan. That could have been the horse the bandit rode, couldn't it?"

Emory Taylor, who was fifty years old and had a little round potbelly and huge handlebar mustaches, nodded emphatically. Rush McErvain, the gun guard, lounged against the wall. He was tall and slat-thin, and one gaunt cheek of his long face bulged with a chew. He squinted his eyes thoughtfully then gave an embarrassed laugh.

"Well, now, Sam, that's something neither one of us can say for sure. The horse was a blue roan, all right, and he looked like a ringer for Gilbert's, if that's what you mean." McErvain worked his jaws twice, looked like he was about to spit, but continued: "Me and Poke Woodman owned a blue roan just about the size of Gilbert's until Poke sold the critter three weeks ago." He laughed reflectively. "You know what Poke did with the money, Johnny. He went on a drunk in town, and you had to run him in until he sobered up. Now the money's gone and the roan's gone. No profit on that deal."

Russell's eyes were slitted. "But you'll swear, Rush, that Gilbert's roan could have been the horse?"

McErvain detached himself from the wall, strolled over to Russell's desk, and spat into the spittoon by Russell's desk. Then McErvain went back to his post at the wall. He planted his shoulders and shrugged. "Could have been."

"All right," said Russell. "Now we'll see how Gilbert looks with these on."

On Russell's desk were an old blue plaid shirt, a worn buckskin jumper, and a gunny sack with eyeholes cut in it. Russell leaned back in his chair and fixed a hard glance on Wade Gilbert.

"Put these on, Gilbert."

Gilbert had been sitting slouched forward in a chair, forearms on his knees, head bowed, while he stared desperately at the floor. It was as if he could feel the penitentiary walls being raised higher and higher around him.

When Russell spoke, Gilbert raised his head and glanced appealingly at Johnny Hull. All Johnny could do was to nod brusquely at the things on Russell's desk. It made Johnny a little sick inside, but he told himself personal feelings had no place in a job like his.

When he saw that Johnny was not going to intervene, Gilbert rose slowly to his feet and began to put on the items on Russell's desk. While he was doing this, Russell said: "Where did you find these things, Johnny?"

"About a mile from where the stage was held up. The clothes were stuffed in the open strongbox."

"You'll testify to that?"

Hull nodded.

Gilbert had the shirt and jumper on. He held the gunny

sack in his hands a moment, as if reluctant to put it over his head, but he finally did so. He stood there looking strange and menacing.

There was silence in the room as all the men stared at Gilbert. Taylor's eyes were squinted thoughtfully. Rush McErvain still lounged against the wall, his jaws working methodically as he worked on his chew. Russell kept glancing, hard-eyed, from Taylor and McErvain to the hooded figure.

Finally Russell snapped: "Well?"

It was Taylor who spoke first. "He's the right size, all right. Put him on the blue roan and I'd say it was the same man. Of course, Sam, I couldn't see under the hood, so I can't swear it was Gilbert."

"Say something, Gilbert," said Russell. "Tell us your name and how many head you have on Twin Bells."

Gilbert complied woodenly.

"Well?" said Russell, staring at Taylor and McErvain. "How's the voice?"

Taylor scratched his chin. "It's muffled under that hood, and, of course, the bandit spoke louder. It could be it."

"What do you say, Rush?" asked Russell.

McErvain's eyes lowered. He stared uncomfortably at the door. "I don't want anybody to get the wrong idea, Sam," he said with obvious reluctance. "Me and Gilbert have never got along too good. I don't want anybody getting the idea I'm trying to put something over on the kid. I'd just as soon stay out of it."

"Nothing doing," snapped Russell. "You were a witness, and it's your duty to get on the stand and tell what you saw. You heard Emory. You saw what happened as well as he did. What do you think of it?"

McErvain made a wry mouth. "I agree. It could have been Gilbert."

"All right. Gilbert," said Russell, "you can take those things off."

Gilbert's face was white as the hood came off. His lips were pinched in helpless anger. "I don't suppose it would do any good to tell you I'm not guilty."

Russell leaned back in the swivel chair. He looked pleased. "It's the judge you should tell that to." He glanced at Johnny Hull. "I'll arrange a hearing with Judge Bradford tomorrow morning, Johnny. I'll let you know when to bring Gilbert. Oh, yes," he said, almost as an afterthought, "he can have a lawyer now if he wants one."

Gilbert looked at Johnny, who nodded at the door. They went out of the prosecutor's office, Gilbert first, and started downstairs. Their boots made hollow, lonely noises on the steps.

Johnny Hull sat at the sheriff's desk, idly twirling a pencil in his fingers. He felt miserable and ill at ease. Old Tom Martin should have been sitting in this chair. Tom Martin should have been shouldering the main responsibility of the sheriff's office, but Martin had a fractured leg and so the business of executing the sheriff's chores had fallen on his deputy. *Of all the rotten luck,* Johnny Hull thought.

The preliminary hearing was over, and Wade Gilbert had been bound over for jury trial. The bond had been set high enough so that Gilbert could not meet it and would have to remain in jail. He was back there in the cell-block now, with his sister Kate visiting him. Johnny Hull dreaded the moment when she left, for she'd pass through the office.

At long last, he heard the swift clicking of her heels as she returned from the cell-block. He could not help throwing a compassionate look at her. He thought he caught the end of a furtive dab at the corners of her eyes, but the glimpse was so fleeting he could not be sure. She stopped, and her glance, when it fell on him, was dry and gelid.

She stood there silently, her mouth pinched, regarding him with scorn and anger. He stirred uncomfortably in his chair. Then he began to fiddle with some papers, hoping he looked absorbed with important business.

It was a while before she spoke, then she said: "Aren't you proud of yourself?"

He didn't know what to say. No matter what he said, she'd probably twist it to mean something different. So he sat, silent and wretched.

"I'll bet you think a lot of yourself," she went on. "Tell me, Mister Hull, how well do you sleep at night?"

Despite the bitter sharpness of her tone, he could sense something more, a deep, hopeless pain in her throat and in her heart. He wanted desperately to help her.

"It's not over yet," he said. "This was just a preliminary hearing. He'll have a jury trial next and a chance to tell his side of it." He paused. "A jury could very well believe him and acquit him." He knew he didn't sound too convincing.

"Who are you trying to fool, cowboy?" she said bitterly. "What can Wade say? That somebody cut our drift fence and hazed some of our stock far up the mountain and he was up there hunting the strays when the hold-up came off? Who's going to believe him, especially when Sam Russell ties into him at the cross-examination? You know Wade won't have a chance."

Johnny knew she was telling the truth. Gilbert's story was weak and without a witness to verify it. Sam Russell had built up a strong case against Wade Gilbert. It made Johnny sick with futility when he thought of it. But he didn't let on to her that he agreed.

"The trial hasn't been held yet," he said, trying to be reassuring. "There's always hope until then."

"Hope? How can there be hope when everyone is against Wade? Who's going to help him? Not Sam Russell. Not you." Her voice was heavy with scorn. "You're too smug and full of self-importance. You're too busy showing off your deputy's star. You . . . you're no more use than a stump in a field!"

With that, she stormed out of the door. Johnny Hull came halfway to his feet, one hand lifting in mute appeal, but she was gone. He sank forlornly back in the chair. Before him he could see the débris of all his shattered dreams.

This high up on the mountain there were still scattered patches of snow under the pines and cedars. Where the sun could get at the ground, the bunch grass was fragrant and green, but under the constant shadow of the trees the snow lay crusted and dirty.

It had been a fruitless search for Johnny Hull, and he began to feel angry at himself for having come up here. He should have known there was nothing to find. Yet he'd had a hope, a foolish, crazy hope of miraculously running across something that would clear Wade Gilbert's name.

From this high point, Hull could look far down the mountain. He could see the road from Arrowhead and the spot where the stagecoach had been held up. In the opposite direction he could stare down on Twin Bells, its buildings toy-like and almost unreal in the distance, and farther, above Twin Bells, he could see the lay-out of Ladder Ranch, which was owned by Rush McErvain and Poke Woodman.

Johnny Hull hardly realized what he was looking at. His mind was occupied with other things. Mostly it was with the feeling of disillusionment and disgust and with a vexation at his own softness. Sentiment had no place in a deputy. It was all right to feel sympathy, but he shouldn't let it lead him to do foolish things.

The evidence all pointed to Wade Gilbert as the road agent, despite Gilbert's denials and those of his sister. Kate was moved by loyalty, which was only normal, and Gilbert, of course, was only trying to get out of it. The best thing for him to do, Johnny Hull thought, was to ride back to Arrowhead and forget all about it. There were other girls in the county besides Kate Gilbert.

But there was the germ of an idea in Johnny Hull's mind. He couldn't define it exactly yet, but it was there, and it wouldn't go, just as the image of Kate Gilbert wouldn't go. *I guess I'm just a soft-hearted damn' fool,* Johnny thought sadly, and urged the sorrel into motion.

He came to Ladder in late afternoon. The air was not so chill down here, and there was no longer any trace of snow, not even beneath the trees or in the shaded hollows. The sorrel circled a corral in which there was a bay and a buckskin, and then Johnny reined in his horse in front of Ladder's house.

He had just swung down to the ground when two men came out. One was Rush McErvain, who padded out his income from Ladder by riding gun guard on the Arrowhead-Fort Benson stage. The other was Poke Woodman, who satisfied himself with the one job of running Ladder.

McErvain showed a smile when he saw Johnny Hull. "Johnny!" he exclaimed. "What brings you to Ladder?"

Johnny shrugged and said nothing. He stared at Poke Woodman, who looked sullen and hostile. He remembered the last time he had seen Woodman. It had been in Arrowhead, and the Ladder man had had a snootful and Johnny had been forced to slam a gun barrel over his head to subdue him enough to put in jail. Johnny supposed Woodman hadn't forgotten about it.

McErvain was working at his chew, his eyes squinted slightly while he stared at Hull. "I saw you come down the mountain. Some trouble up there?"

"Just looking around," said Johnny Hull. He resented McErvain's patronizing manner. McErvain spoke as if he were only a child who didn't know his way around.

"Looking around?" echoed McErvain. He spat in the dirt in front of him. "Looking around for what?"

"A blue roan," said Hull.

In the silence a jay chattered raucously. One of the horses in the corral whinnied, and Johnny's sorrel answered. McErvain and Woodman exchanged looks. Woodman scowled. McErvain's brows were lifted as if either in surprise or amusement.

"A blue roan?" said McErvain gently. "Why, did Gilbert's critter get away from you?" He shook his head reprovingly. "That's bad, son. That blue roan is state's evidence."

"I'm not talking about Gilbert's roan," said Hull.

"Oh?" said McErvain softly. Woodson darted another glance at him, but McErvain didn't acknowledge it. He spat a large spot on the ground not two feet from Hull's boots. "That's the only blue roan in the county. What else could you mean, son?"

"Quit calling me son!"

"Oh?" McErvain grinned. "What you so hot about . . . son?"

"You're the one that's gonna be hot in a few minutes," growled Johnny.

Woodman spoke up, sounding cold and irate. "If you mean the blue roan me and Rush had, we sold the critter. Three, four weeks ago, it was." His scowl darkened. "You should remember."

Johnny Hull's lips were stiff. His heart was banging away

inside him. "I'd like to see your receipt," he said.

"You callin' me a liar?" snarled Woodman.

McErvain still smiled. "Go get the receipt, Poke," he said. "He's the law, you know. We don't want trouble with the law."

While Woodman was gone in the house, Rush McErvain kept that smug and condescending smile on his face. Johnny was getting furious, but he forced himself to calm down. He'd only be playing into their hands if he lost his head.

Woodman came back with a slip of paper in his hand. Scowling, he shoved it at Johnny. "I don't know if you can read," he said jeeringly. "If you can, you'll see that it's signed by J. Hewitt from Palo Pinto, Texas."

"I wouldn't get too smart if I was you," Johnny murmured. He studied the paper a moment, then handed it back to Woodman. "I'll have to send a wire to Palo Pinto and see if there's a J. Hewitt from the town."

"You still callin' me a liar?"

McErvain lifted a deterring hand to Woodman. McErvain's eyes were narrowed a little as he stared at Johnny.

"We only took the man's word he was from Palo Pinto," McErvain said. "If this Hewitt's not from there, it doesn't mean a damn' thing. The man paid us money, good money, which was all we was really interested in. You know what Poke did with his share." McErvain's voice hardened. "You're young, Johnny, and we'll overlook it this time, but don't go crowding us. We don't like what you're insinuatin'. Gilbert's your man. Don't go trying to frame what he done on someone else."

"I'm not trying to frame anybody," said Johnny. "I'm just trying to find out the truth." His glance was cold as he laid it on Poke Woodman. "Where were you at the time the stage was held up, Poke?"

"Right here at Ladder. Can you prove I wasn't?"

"I think so," said Hull quietly.

Woodman made an angry sound deep in his throat. His right hand poised above the handle of his gun, but McErvain stuck out that restraining hand again.

"Don't be a fool, Poke," he said sharply. "The kid's only bluffing."

"We'll see if I'm bluffing." Johnny tried to say it with conviction. He knew a moment's fear, for he realized that he could very well get himself killed.

He tried telling himself Kate Gilbert wasn't worth dying for, but then it occurred to him he had a duty that far transcended anything he owed to Kate Gilbert—his duty to see that an innocent man did not suffer for another's crime. That was every lawman's duty, over and beyond any personal feelings he might have. Johnny Hull's lips tightened to resolution.

"You're Gilbert's size, Poke," Johnny went on. "Your voice under a gunny sack could pass for Gilbert's. What would a jury think when Gilbert's lawyer dresses you up in the bandit's clothes?"

The corners of Woodman's mouth pulled down. Again McErvain touched Woodman's gun arm.

"Don't let him rile you, Poke," said McErvain. "That don't mean a thing. I could dig up twenty men in the county of Gilbert's size. Put the bandit's clothes on all of them and no one could tell the difference." His eyes glittered as he stared at Hull. "It's the blue roan that cinches Gilbert's guilt, Johnny . . . the only blue roan in the county."

"What if I can prove it isn't the only blue roan?"

"What are you drivin' at?"

Johnny Hull's throat was dry. He could feel the sweat coursing down his sides and his neck.

"What if I can dig up your blue roan, Rush?" he said, with as much certainty as he could put into his voice. "What if I can dig him up with a bullet in him and then prove there never was a J. Hewitt?"

Woodman cried: "He knows too much, Rush! I'll fix him. . . ."

"Wait, Poke!" shouted McErvain. "He's bluffin', I tell you. . . ."

But Poke Woodman, carried away by his rage, was no longer to be restrained. He jerked his right arm free and grabbed at his gun. Johnny Hull knew it was coming. He had deliberately brought it about and that was the only advantage he had. He was prepared for it, and his gun came into his hand and he fired at the instant that Woodman's .45 leveled.

Johnny knew he had hit Woodman, but there was still McErvain. The moment he fired, Johnny leaped to the side and crouched. He heard McErvain's weapon explode. The slug whined wickedly past his ear, and then his own gun was cracking again.

The slug took McErvain in the shoulder and spun him around. He screamed in pain, and the gun went flying from his fingers. He sank to his knees, clutching his shattered shoulder.

Swiftly Johnny swung his gun back to Woodman. But there no longer was anything to fear from him. He lay flat on his back, staring with widespread eyes at the sky.

Johnny walked over to McErvain and picked up the man's gun. McErvain began to curse him until he saw the look on Johnny's face. Then he subsided.

Rage and reaction shook Johnny's voice. "You thought because Tom Martin was laid up and I was a young, dumb deputy, you and Poke could put one over, didn't you? You planned it out in advance. You pretended to sell the blue roan three weeks before the hold-up so the blame would fall on Wade Gilbert. After the hold-up, you killed the roan and buried it. You thought I was too dumb to figure it out."

"You were bluffin'," snarled McErvain. "You never found our roan."

"That's right," agreed Johnny Hull. "But now I know it's buried somewhere. If it wasn't, Poke never would have tried to kill me. Even if you won't tell me where, I'll find it. I promise you that."

Johnny Hull was seated at Tom Martin's desk when he heard the footsteps enter the office. They sounded timid and hesitant, and he looked up and saw Kate Gilbert standing there. There was a stunned look in her eyes, and her fingers kept twining about each other.

"Yes?" he said as coldly as he could.

"I'm sorry, Johnny. If you never speak to me again, I won't blame you. But I am sorry for the way I treated you and for what I said to you. I want you to know I'll never bother you again. Good bye, Johnny." She turned to leave.

He said sharply: "Wait!"

She paused, eyes lowered. He found it hard to suppress a grin. Still he managed to speak very sternly.

"I might want to come out to Twin Bells sometime in the future. I'm telling you now that, when I do, I won't stand for any doors slammed in my face or any dishwater thrown at me. Understand?"

"I understand," she murmured.

"All right," he said. "You can go now."

In the doorway she halted. "You coming out to Twin Bells. How . . . soon would that be? I . . . I'm sure Wade would like to know."

"Tell Wade I'll be out Saturday evening." He paused.

"You can tag along if you want to."

"Oh, I want to . . . very much."

Then she was gone. Johnny Hull settled back in the sheriff's chair and a feeling of great contentment came over him.

The Scalp Hunters

The Indian girl got on at Silver Springs. The coach was ready to get under way when she came around a corner of the station and mutely showed her ticket to the driver. He leaned down and took it and waited for her to get in.

Bannister, sitting alone on the front seat, reached over and opened the door for her. Sternwood and Donlin, seated across from him, watched—Donlin with sudden hostility and Sternwood with idle interest. The girl threw one swift look up and around as she stepped in. Then her eyes dropped, and she took a seat next to Bannister. The coach started with a jerk that made her lurch forward, but she caught at the windowsill and steadied herself.

Bannister stared out of his window as the coach pulled away. A pinto pony stood beside the stage station with drooping head. Caked lather stained its flanks. It was obvious the animal had come a long way, and hard. There was no saddle or bridle, only a hackamore, which made it an Indian pony. Was it the girl's?

The coach rocked and lurched, squealing on its thoroughbraces as it rattled down the rutted, dusty street. Then the adobe buildings of Silver Springs lay behind, and ahead were the burning hills of sand and scrub and desolation.

With nothing to occupy his mind other than the tedious journey ahead, Bannister found his thoughts reverting to the Indian pony. There was some significance about it he could not grasp. Even the exact nature of it eluded him. But in the back of his mind was a vague uneasiness that left him faintly troubled.

He settled back, seeking as comfortable a position as he could against the hard back of the seat, and got himself attuned to the rocking rhythm of the coach. The Indian girl was tense, sitting bolt upright and jerking violently with each sway of the coach. Her hand gripped the windowsill so hard her knuckles showed white against the dark texture of her skin.

It was obvious to Bannister that she had never ridden in a stage before.

"Relax," he said. "Don't fight it. Just go along with it like I'm doing."

The girl stared straight ahead, giving no indication that she had heard or understood.

"Relaje," he said in Spanish. "*¿Compredeme?* Do you understand?"

She turned and looked at him. Her eyes were wide and luminous, but he doubted this was from fright. Her tribal group knew no fear. It was more of a childish wonder, and awe.

He smiled at her. "Sit like I am sitting," he told her in Spanish. "It is nothing, once you become accustomed to it."

She obeyed gradually, as though not trusting him or the rocking coach. But she finally settled in a corner, as far from him as she could. For a little while she was like that, staring straight ahead while picking up the rhythm of the coach. After that she threw one look at Bannister. If there was gratitude in it, he could not tell. The agate sheen of her dark eyes revealed nothing.

"What tribe would you say she's from?" Sternwood asked. "All Indians look alike to me."

"Apache," Donlin said. He made the word sound vile.

"Is that so?" Sternwood remarked. "She doesn't look very savage to me." He tightened his saffron duster about his throat to keep dust from soiling his clothing. The fact that this made him sweat seemed not to matter to him. He evidently preferred an immaculate suit to personal discomfort.

"Is it true what they say about the Apaches," he asked, "that they're the most cruel of all?"

"They're mean, all right," Donlin said. He scratched at his dusty stubble of whiskers, and his small, red-rimmed eyes glared with a sudden hate. "Dirty, stinkin' Injuns!" he spat.

Sternwood seemed amused. "I take it you don't admire Apaches, Donlin."

"Not just Apaches. I hate all Injuns."

"Ever killed any?"

"I've killed my share."

"Doesn't it bother you?"

Donlin snorted. "Not Injuns. They bother me less than killing a snake."

Some private amusement heightened in Sternwood's eyes. "Aren't you afraid she might understand you, Donlin?"

"She doesn't understand English. Even if she did, I wouldn't worry. I ain't scared of Injuns . . . not even dirty, stinkin' Apaches."

Sternwood looked questioningly at Bannister. "Was that Spanish you spoke to her?" he asked.

Bannister nodded.

"Isn't that strange? That they should know Spanish, I mean."

Bannister stared at the man. "Aren't you from the Southwest?"

Sternwood laughed easily, with amusement still glinting in his eyes. "What makes you ask that? I'm on my way from California to my home in the East . . . Philadelphia. The sun shines in California, too, Bannister."

"And Spanish is spoken in California," Bannister pointed out.

"I'm aware of that, but I spent most of my time in Frisco, where there aren't many Spanish-speaking people." Sternwood's laugh held a hint of embarrassment. "I play at cards, you see," he said.

Bannister made no comment. He turned his gaze outside, to the bleak and barren landscape passing by.

"How is it Apaches know Spanish?" Sternwood asked after an interval, and, when Bannister looked at him, he laughed quietly and continued. "I don't mean to annoy you, Bannister. I'm just trying to make conversation. But this is my first time in the Southwest, and I'm naturally curious. We hear a lot about the Apaches . . . even in California."

"How did you get to Frisco?"

"By ship. I crossed the Isthmus of Panama and then took another ship." He turned his attention back to the Indian girl, who still stared straight ahead, into a world of her own that excluded all of them. "It seems strange to me that she should know Spanish and not English."

"The Apaches here always ranged on both sides of the border," said Bannister. "They speak Spanish as well as their native tongues. Many of them have Spanish names, such as Victorio."

"Would you say she's from Mexico?"

Bannister shrugged. "You know as much about that as I do."

Sternwood's eyes narrowed ever so slightly. The amusement in their depths flickered and faded. "I don't understand what you mean," he said.

"Don't you?"

"How could I?"

Bannister glanced at the girl who still sat apart, without sign that she understood him. Something about her disturbed him. Was her indifference too studied, too preoccupied? But all Indians had the knack of seeming distant and apart, like a spire of rock or one of the lonely Joshua trees outside.

What are you jumpy about? Bannister asked himself. *Is it the money belt around your waist . . . the pay for that herd you delivered in Tacoma? If you are going to fear anyone, fear Donlin. He looks like the type who would rob you for a dime. . . .*

He slouched down in the seat and pulled his hat over his eyes. It took a little while, but finally he began to doze.

The stop was called Pearl. Whoever had christened it had been prompted either by sentimental recollection of a loved one or by a macabre sense of humor. There was the station and corrals and a shed, and that was all. Even the presence of water, which accounted for the stage station, was not enough to lure anyone else into settling here. The hills were rugged and brown, and in the distance mountains loomed, blue and mystical. In between them was lonesomeness and desolation.

While the horses were changed, the passengers refreshed themselves as best they could. Donlin splashed water on his face, the back of his neck, and his hairy forearms, not so much to cleanse himself as for the cooling effect. Sternwood watched with patent disapproval. He had removed his duster, fustian, and tie, and had opened his shirt at the throat and rolled up the sleeves. He looked out of place in this frontier setting—except for the ivory-handled pistol in the holster at his side.

He glanced at the Indian girl who stood at some distance away, staring off at the blue-hazed mountains. His soft, apologetic laugh was starting to get on Bannister's nerves.

"Even though she's an Apache," Sternwood said, "I feel uncomfortable. Modesty, you know. But I dare say she is accustomed to men wearing much less than this. I understand

Apache men run around with little on. Is that true?"

Bannister grunted.

"You aren't very sociable, are you?" Sternwood said, but all his softness of speech could not quite conceal the thin edge of steel in his voice.

"I've never been much for talk," said Bannister.

"I wouldn't bother you," Sternwood murmured, "but there's no one else to talk to. The girl speaks only Spanish, and Donlin is . . . well, he's lacking in conversational abilities, to say the least."

Donlin was done now, and Sternwood took his turn. Afterward he went into the stage station, while Bannister washed. Bannister had a drink of cold water at the pump, and then stood in the shade of the station building. He did not go inside because he had already had enough of Sternwood's conversation.

He wondered at the faint uneasiness that remained with him. He recalled the pinto pony and the impression it had made on him. Why? All at once he remembered having seen another pinto at Elsburg, the stop before Silver Springs—a black and white pinto that could have been the same one. But even if had been the same one, what could it portend?

Now that the men had left, the Indian girl went to the pump. Bannister watched her, noting the lithe grace with which she moved. She was wearing a loose red blouse and a long, billowing black skirt, but even these could not conceal the hint of a slim, lissome body. The wind whipped her long black hair as she bent to drink.

Bannister watched, and all at once a cold sense of foreboding struck through him. She had filled the tin dipper, but she did not drink from it. Instead, she took a small, hollow reed from her beaded bag tied to her waist, and through this reed she sucked water.

* * * * *

They sat as before, Bannister and the Apache girl with their backs to the front of the coach and, facing them, Donlin and Sternwood. Donlin sat with his wide-brimmed hat over his face and his arms crossed over his chest in an attempt at sleep. But Sternwood showed no fatigue. He sat swaying effortlessly with each movement of the coach, with that secret again in his eyes.

"What part of Mexico would you say she's from?" he asked abruptly, nodding at the girl.

It was Donlin who answered. "The east flank of the Sierra Madre. That's Apache country. The Yaquis are on the west side." He did not remove the hat from his face.

"I thought you were asleep," Sternwood said.

"I never sleep," Donlin said, "not when there's a dirty, stinking Apache around."

Sternwood's laugh held polite contempt. "Do you mean you're afraid of a girl?"

Donlin took the hat from his face. Red-rimmed eyes glared at Sternwood. "I ain't afraid of no Injun, but that don't mean I have to be a damned fool when one's around."

"You ever been in Apache country?" Sternwood asked.

"We're in Apache country right now."

"Oh? Well, I didn't mean that. I meant Mexico."

"I've been there."

"Is that why you're afraid?"

Donlin's hand moved to his side. "You accusin' me of being afraid of a dirty Injun?"

Sternwood laughed apologetically. "You said you'd been in Apache country. Didn't you admit you've killed Indians? What part of Mexico is Apache country, anyway?"

"I already told you."

"I didn't mean the Sierra Madre. I meant what state. Chihuahua? Sonora?"

Bannister said: "I thought you didn't know anything about Apaches."

Sternwood's glance cooled. "I don't," he said. "But I do have a knowledge of geography. I merely assume it would be one of those states, since they are both east of the Sierra Madre."

"There are Apaches in Durango and Coahuila, too," Bannister said, staring hard at Sternwood.

Sternwood stared back at him guilelessly. "Oh? You seem to know a lot about Apaches, too, Bannister. Where did you say you're from?"

"I've got a ranch out of Las Cruces, but I've been through most of the Southwest. I've known Mescaleros, Jicarillas, and Chiricahuas. I've known them all."

"Mescaleros? Chiricahuas? What are those?"

"Apaches."

"You mean there are different kinds of Apaches?"

"Didn't you know?"

Sternwood spread his hands. "How could I? I'm a stranger passing through this country."

"You talk like an educated man. That's why I thought you knew."

Embarrassment tinged Sternwood's soft laugh. "Thank you, I'm flattered." His glance moved to the girl again. "What state in Mexico would you say she's from?"

"I don't know."

"Why don't you ask her?"

"She could be from any, and from this side of the border, as well. Apaches are nomads. At one time or another, she may have lived in every one of those states and in Arizona and New Mexico, too."

"Ask her name, then."

"Why do you want to know?"

Sternwood shrugged. "It might turn out to be something picturesque, or amusing. Go ahead and ask her, Bannister."

Bannister looked at the girl. There was no liking in him for this, but he thought he would humor the man. "How are you called?" he asked in Spanish.

The girl's head turned slowly. She stared at Bannister without speaking, dark eyes and impassive features revealing nothing, not even whether she had heard. Bannister glanced at the beaded bag fastened to her waist, remembering how she had drunk water through a hollow reed.

"How are you called?" he asked again.

It looked as though she would not answer this time, either. Finally her lips moved. "Magdalena," she said, her voice low, throaty.

"Magdalena?" Sternwood echoed. "Would that be Magdalene in English? What a quaint name for a savage! I told you it might be something picturesque." His glance shifted to the lonely landscape beyond his window. "What's the next stop?"

"Cerro Alto."

"Is it a town?"

"A village. We'll be there overnight."

Sternwood brushed at the soiled sleeve of his duster. "What a tedious, filthy journey! I should have returned by way of Panama. But jungle or desert doesn't give a man much choice, does it, Bannister?"

Bannister was thinking of a lather-streaked pony, of a girl drinking water through a reed, and trying to tie it all into something understandable.

"I couldn't say, Sternwood," he replied. "I've never seen a jungle."

He could not sleep. The wind was moaning, and a loose

shutter was banging somewhere on Urban's roadhouse here at the edge of the tiny settlement. But it was not this that kept him awake. It was an intuition of great peril.

Unable to shake the feeling, he dressed and went outside. He stood in the yard, breathing the bitter wind and listening to its ancient, secret voice. The money belt pressed uncomfortably about his middle. Was it the money he was carrying that made him so uneasy?

Donlin was not a man to be trifled with, and Sternwood, despite his almost ceaseless talk, struck Bannister as even more dangerous. They had sought to get him in a poker game earlier that evening, and he had pleaded lack of money. But he was sure Sternwood had not believed him.

Did it have something to do with the girl's drinking through a reed? He knew what that meant—but she was a girl, not an Apache warrior. Why hadn't she gotten on the stage at Elsburg? He was sure now that she had been there, and she had ridden her pinto pony nearly to death to catch the coach at Silver Springs. Were there Apache warriors out in the night, awaiting some signal from her?

Bannister did not think so. There was a moon and stars, and in their frigid light the *jacales* of Cerro Alto slept the deceptively peaceful sleep of all inanimate things. No, this was something more malevolent. He knew he had the answer in him but could not draw it out, and this inability left him irritable. In silent exasperation, he went back inside.

By now his eyes were attuned to the darkness and immediately spotted the lurking figure before the door of Donlin's room. Whoever it was appeared so intent on listening that Bannister's approach went undetected until one of his boots squeaked faintly.

There was a whirl of movement, an upflung arm, and Bannister drove in fast to grab the wrist before it could strike. The wrist was small, even dainty, and this and the odor of camp smoke told him who it was.

"Magdalena," he whispered, "it's Bannister."

The only sound she made was the swift running of her breath. She remained tense, her fingers never slackening their grip on the knife although he squeezed her wrist tightly.

"What are you up to?" he demanded, still whispering. "What are you trying to do?"

She began to subside. Her breathing slowed, the tenseness started to ebb in her, and she no longer strained at his grip.

"These are dangerous men," he whispered, relaxing a little. "If you mean to steal and they catch you, it will go bad for you."

The instant his grip relented, she jerked free. She stepped back, the knife menacing him.

"I do not mean to steal," she hissed. "I mean to kill . . . and, if you get in my way again, I will kill you!"

The amusement in Sternwood's eyes was wry and cold today. He was silent, although it was not from a loss of words. He gave the impression that this was a self-imposed silence while his mind contended with other things. Donlin slouched sullenly beside him, silent as well.

Bannister, too, was quiet, immersed in grave, profound thinking. All of the fragments, the insinuations of memory and knowledge had fallen together, and a picture had formed with chilling clarity.

The Indian girl had drunk through a reed. Now he remembered that she had surreptitiously scratched her head with a tiny stick, and the significance of these acts lay naked and menacing in his mind. The first four times an Apache warrior went on the warpath, he was forbidden to let water touch his lips or to scratch his head with his fingers. So he used a hollow reed to drink and a tiny stick to scratch.

But Magdalena was a girl. What could be her motive? Bannister thought he knew, and he was left with a feeling of disgust and shame for his race.

Sternwood spoke for the first time.

"Our savage friend isn't with us today. Was Cerro Alto her destination, Bannister?"

Bannister shrugged and said nothing.

"I had the impression she was going much farther," Sternwood persisted. "What made her change her mind?"

"Why? Are you worried?"

"Worried?" Sternwood asked. "What makes you say that?"

"Didn't you notice that she drank through a reed?" Bannister asked. "Whenever a young Apache does that, he's on the warpath."

"So?"

"Just thought I'd mention it," Bannister replied, aware that Donlin was watching him closely.

"Why would she be on the warpath?" Sternwood asked.

"Have you ever taken scalps, Donlin?"

Donlin straightened very slowly, with the ominous lethargy of a huge, aroused bear. Red-rimmed eyes blinked once then stared, unmoving.

"What if I have? I only gave the dirty, stinking Injuns a taste of their own medicine."

"Comanche and Apache scalps?" Bannister asked.

Donlin's grunt neither admitted nor denied.

"In Mexico?"

"Was I the first white man to take scalps?" Donlin growled. "Was I the only one? Maybe you've scalped Injuns, too, Bannister?"

"No," Bannister said slowly. "I never have. But if I ever do, it won't be for pay."

Sternwood was bending forward, his eyes very bright. "Go on," he urged. "This interests me."

"Does it?"

"I mean the taking of scalps for pay. I never heard of it. When was this and where?"

"Not so long ago," Bannister said, "the states of Durango, Chihuahua, Sonora, and Coahuila offered bounties for Comanche and Apache scalps . . . two hundred *pesos* for males, one hundred and fifty for females, and one hundred for children alive so they could be enslaved. Some American renegades made quite a business of it until they went too far and started turning in Mexican scalps as Indian."

Sternwood was tense with a strange excitement. "And this girl . . . you think she is one of those Apaches?"

"She could be."

"And she is out for revenge?" Sternwood settled back in his seat. "Well, I've never been in Mexico. What about you, Donlin?"

"You calling me a scalp hunter?" Donlin was sitting bolt upright, his hand on his pistol.

Sternwood's laugh was soft and unintimidated. "I thought you were afraid of her, even though she is just a girl. Now that I know why, I don't blame you. In your boots I'd be afraid, too."

A dry arroyo made a small arc about this stop, which was called Thorpe, and in the bend lay the station and the corrals. There was no other structure. Nothing else was visible except the looming mountains all around, and the green patches of piñon and scrub cedar. In the thin air the sounds made by the hostlers and driver as they changed horses rang sharply clear.

She stood at the very edge of the small stand of nut pines that lined the lip of the arroyo. Sternwood and Donlin saw her the same instant Bannister did. The two glanced at each other, and one said something so quickly and softly that Bannister did not hear. Then they started toward the girl. When she saw them, she drew a knife from beneath her skirt. The blade flashed in the sun.

"Just a minute!" Bannister called. "Where are you going?"

They stopped. Sternwood turned slightly, but his glance remained on the girl. Donlin swung around, facing Bannister.

"You taking a hand in this, Bannister?" he shouted.

"Leave her alone," said Bannister.

"She'll hound us," snarled Donlin. "You think I want to wake up some morning with a knife between my ribs?"

"Why didn't you think of that when you were taking scalps?"

"Why, you dirty Injun lover!" Donlin screamed, and went for his gun.

Bannister drew quickly and fired. The bullet rocked Donlin, but he did not go down. He steadied himself and brought his pistol to bear on Bannister. Bannister followed with a second shot that slammed Donlin back. His feet tangled, and he went down. He was dead and did not know it when he hit the ground.

Bannister, tense and alert, swept a swift glance, seeking Sternwood. He saw the man disappearing into the piñons, gun in hand. The girl was nowhere in sight.

Bannister started ahead cautiously, entering the trees with his heart racing. He did not dare proceed fast. He moved from tree to tree, with a feeling of urgency building up inside him.

The scream, when it came, brought Bannister to an abrupt

halt. His flesh crawled. The scream persisted, longer than it seemed possible, full of frenzied terror and insufferable anguish. When it ended, its memory rang through the forest like an echo of evil.

Bannister went on and found Sternwood lying face down on the ground, with a pool of blood fanning out beneath him. There was a small pool near his head, formed by the bleeding wound where his scalp had been.

Bannister turned and went back quickly the way he'd come.

One of the hostlers held a rifle on Bannister while the driver, upon the seat, said: "You're not riding in my coach another mile, bucko. I don't care what your ticket says. I don't haul anyone that sides with an Apache."

"They meant to kill her," Bannister said. "You saw them."

The driver yelled and cracked his whip, and the coach was off. The hostler wagged his rifle.

"Git!" he said to Bannister.

"At least sell me a horse. I'll pay."

"Git!"

He began walking. He topped the rise and glanced back at Thorpe. They were still watching him, and there was nothing to do but move on. Dust curled from under his boots. The bitter desert wind whispered, mocking him.

The sound of hoof beats a while later brought him swinging around, jerking his pistol. Then he saw that it was the Apache girl, and she was alone.

She had a coyote dun that she had probably stolen in Cerro Alto. "You may ride with me," she said, her face grave and emotionless, "until we can steal a horse for you."

A piece of bloody flesh and hair dangled from her waist. Her skirt was spotted with blood. Bannister could not suppress a shudder. "Did you have to do that?" he asked, pointing to the scalp.

"How else are my people to know that he is dead?"

"They were scalp hunters, then? Both of them?"

"The Donlin I do not know," she said. "The Sternwood, yes."

"Are you sure?"

"He wore a beard in those days, but I remembered him. He was the leader. He was the one who took the scalps of my father and mother and brother."

"And you?" Bannister asked.

"I was young and so I was sold, but I escaped. Are you coming? I will stay with you until you find a horse. Then I must return to my people with the news."

He got on the dun behind her. She kicked the horse with her heels, and the dun moved on across the lonely land, into the cruel vastness of desolation, into the ancient home of ancestral fury.

About the Author

H(enry) A(ndrew) DeRosso was born on July 15, 1917 in Carey, Wisconsin. In the decades between 1940 and 1960 he published approximately two hundred Western short stories and short novels in various pulp magazines, known for their dark and compelling visions of the night side of life and their austere realism. He was also the author of six Western novels, perhaps the most notable of which are .44 (1953) and THE DARK BRAND (1963). He died on October 14, 1960.

About the Editor

Bill Pronzini was born in Petaluma, California. His earliest Western fiction was published under his own name and a variety of pseudonyms in *Zane Grey Western Magazine*. Among his most notable Western novels are STARVATION CAMP (1984) and FIREWIND (1989). A collection of his short stories, ALL THE LONG YEARS, will be published by Five Star Westerns in 2001. He is also the editor of numerous Western story collections, including UNDER THE BURNING SUN: WESTERN STORIES (Five Star Westerns, 1997) by H. A. DeRosso and RENEGADE RIVER: WESTERN STORIES (Five Star Westerns, 1998) by Giff Cheshire. He is married to author Marcia Muller. They make their home in Petaluma.